Allan B. Magruder

John Marshall

Volume 1

Allan B. Magruder

John Marshall
Volume 1

ISBN/EAN: 9783337381110

Printed in Europe, USA, Canada, Australia, Japan

Cover: Foto ©Andreas Hilbeck / pixelio.de

More available books at **www.hansebooks.com**

American Statesmen

JOHN MARSHALL

BY

ALLAN B. MAGRUDER

BOSTON AND NEW YORK
HOUGHTON, MIFFLIN AND COMPANY
The Riverside Press, Cambridge

The Riverside Press, Cambridge, Mass., U. S. A.
Electrotyped and Printed by H. O. Houghton & Company.

PREFACE.

THE great fame of John Marshall, as Chief Justice of the United States, has so far overshadowed the remembrance of his other services to his countrymen, as to render many of them oblivious of his public career as soldier, legislator, envoy, historian, and statesman, both previous to and after his elevation to the first place on the Supreme Bench. These pages are designed to supply these almost forgotten features of his active, busy life, in addition to sketching his more familiar career on the bench.

The author has received material aid from the immediate descendants and family connections of the Chief Justice, the admirable memorial discourse of Judge Story, and the excellent memoir by Mr. Horace Binney of the Philadelphia Bar. He is also largely indebted to the industry and discriminating research of

Mr. Henry Flanders, in his "Lives and Times of the Chief Justices," of which he has freely availed himself for facts and incidents which lend interest to the narrative.

STEPHENS CITY, VIRGINIA.

CONTENTS.

JOHN MARSHALL.

CHAPTER I.

YOUTH.

JOHN MARSHALL was born on the 24th day of September in the year 1755, at German-town, a roadside village in what was then the frontier county of Fauquier in the colony of Virginia; the place is now known as *Midland*, a station on the Virginia Midland Railroad. Attaining his majority in 1776, he entered active life at an eventful period. Colonel Thomas Marshall, his father, was born in the county of Westmoreland in Virginia, in what is still known as the Northern Neck, — a peninsula thus named by reason of its location between those bold and beautiful rivers, the Potomac and the Rappahannock. Of this country the late Governor Barbour of Virginia was wont to say: "It is the prolific soil that grows presidents," — in allusion to the fact that when these words were uttered Westmoreland had

1

contributed to the national service Washington, Madison, and Monroe, three out of the five persons who up to that time had held that rank.

What Boston was to Massachusetts, Westmoreland was to the other counties of Virginia; the birth-place and the home of the Washingtons, the Lees, the Masons, the Taliaferros, the Marshalls, the Madisons, the Monroes, the Graysons, the Roanes, the Beverlys, the Bankheads, the Balls, the McCartys, the Blands, and the Carters, it became a sentinel on the watch-tower of liberty, — the herald to announce the approach of danger. It was here that the friends of freedom first perceived the danger-signal, as early as 1765, the date of the first stamp act. They drew up the earliest Declaration of colonial rights, which was written by Richard Henry Lee, whose name, signed first upon the page, is followed by one hundred and fourteen others of the chief men of the county. This is said to have been the first public association in the land for resistance to that act.[1]

The Marshall family were of British descent, having emigrated from Wales to the colonies. They were distinguished by their intellect and force of character. The grandfather of the

[1] See Bp. Meade's *Old Families of Virginia*, vol. ii. p. 434, Appendix.

Chief Justice was John Marshall, who left four sons, the most distinguished of whom was Thomas, father of the great judge, whose talents and character gave him a high rank in the colony. He was born in 1732, the year of Washington's birth, and was sent to school at the academy of Archibald Campbell, a Scotchman, descended from a branch of the family of the Duke of Argyle, a clergyman of the Episcopal Church, and a thorough scholar. Thomas Marshall became a land surveyor, and accompanied Washington, who was his neighbor and had been his school-mate, in his surveying expeditions for Lord Fairfax. He was afterward a lieutenant of Virginia troops in the French war, and was present at the defeat of Braddock. He was several times elected to the Virginia House of Burgesses, never failing to obtain the suffrages of the people, whose respect and confidence he held in the fullest measure ; and he warmly participated in all the earliest movements to encourage the colonists in resistance to British tyranny. When the call to arms was made in Virginia, he was one of the first to offer his services, and was a field officer of the first regiment raised. In his first engagement, at the battle of the Great Bridge in 1775 with a detachment of British troops under Lord Dunmore, he was distinguished for

valor and good conduct. Afterwards he suc-
cessively commanded in the Continental line
the Third Virginia Infantry and the First Virginia Artillery, as their colonel, serving most
of the time with Woodford's brigade. He was
in the battles of Germantown and Brandywine,
having three horses killed under him, and in
the latter engagement contributed largely by
his courage and skill to save the American
army. He endured, with three of his sons, all
the hardships of the winter campaign at Valley
Forge. Subsequently he was ordered to join
the southern army, and with a part of his regiment he was taken prisoner at Charleston.
During the term of his parole he made his first
visit to Kentucky through the wilderness, in
1780. Returning to Virginia, he remained to
the close of the war, and in 1785 emigrated
with the younger members of his family to Kentucky, near Versailles, in Woodford County,
which he procured to be named Woodford;
after his old friend and commander. In the
early history of Kentucky he bore a scarce less
active, distinguished and patriotic part than he
had done in his native State. He died in 1806
at the home of his son, Captain Thomas Marshall, in Mason County, and lies buried in the
family cemetery near Washington, in that
State.

In token of his great bravery and patriotic services, Colonel Marshall was presented by Edmund Randolph, Attorney General in Washington's cabinet, and also Governor of Virginia, with a splendid sword, now in possession of one of his descendants in Kentucky, and preserved as a precious heir-loom in the family.

The wife of Colonel Thomas Marshall was Mary Isham Keith. Her father, James Keith, was an Episcopal minister, and cousin-german to the last Earl Marischal and to Field-Marshal James Keith, one of the most valued of the great Frederick's lieutenants, who saved the Prussian army and fell at Hochkirch, "as poor as a Scot, though he had had the ransoming of three cities."

Of the mother of the Chief Justice we know but little more than that she bore fifteen children, — seven sons and eight daughters, — and that she reared them all to mature years. She could have had little opportunity to make any other record for herself, and could hardly have made a better one. Of the fifteen, John Marshall was the first born. The date of the removal of Colonel Thomas Marshall from Westmoreland to Fauquier is not certainly known. It must have been soon after his marriage, for his son John was born, as we have seen, at Germantown in Fauquier, in 1755. Subsequently he acquired, and moved to, the fine estate of Oak Hill, in another part of the same county, which continued to be the seat of the Marshall family up to a recent date. Colonel Marshall was a gentleman of intelligence and plain education, and devoted himself personally to the training of his children. He had a private teacher from Scotland, a Mr. James Thompson, a clergyman, who came to this country and took up his residence in the family of Colonel Marshall in 1767, and instructed his sons, John and James, and others.

Of Colonel Thomas Marshall, Judge Story, deriving his information from contemporary sources, says: "He was a man of uncommon capacity and vigor of intellect, and though his original education was imperfect, he overcame this disadvantage by the diligence and perseverance with which he cultivated his natural endowments; so that he soon acquired, and maintained throughout the course of his life, among associates of no mean character, the reputation of masculine sense and extraordinary ability. No better proof indeed need be adduced to justify this opinion than the fact that he possessed the unbounded confidence, respect, and admiration of all his children at that mature period of their lives when they were fully able to appreciate his worth and to compare and measure him with other men of known eminence. I have often heard the Chief Justice speak of him in terms of the deepest affection and reverence. I do not here refer to his public remarks, but to his private and familiar conversations with me, when there was no other listener. Indeed, he never named his father on these occasions without dwelling on his character with a fond and winning enthusiasm. It was a theme on which he broke out with a spontaneous eloquence; and in the spirit of the most persuasive confidence, he would delight to expatiate upon his virtues and talents. 'My father' (would he say with kindled feelings and emphasis) 'my father was a far abler man than any of his sons. To him I owe the solid foundation of all my own success in life.'" [1]

John Marshall early evinced a strong love for English literature, especially in the departments of poetry and history. At the early age of twelve it is said that he knew by heart a large portion of Pope's writings and had made himself familiar with Dryden, Shakespeare, and Milton. Subsequently, at the age of fourteen, he was sent to school in Westmoreland County, to the classical academy of the Messrs. Campbell, in which formerly his father and General

[1] *Discourse on the Life of Marshall*, p. 9.

Washington had been pupils, and where James Monroe was one of his fellow-students. Returning home at the end of his term, he continued his study of Latin, reading Horace and Livy. He pursued these studies under the direction of his old preceptor, Mr. Thompson, who was an accomplished classicist. Fortunately he was also fond of athletic sports and exercises in the open air. He began the study of law at the age of eighteen; but the impending struggle with Great Britain so absorbed his mind as to interrupt his studies before he had obtained a license to practice. He joined a company of volunteers, and by precept and example stimulated the spirit of resistance to British oppression.

CHAPTER II.

MILITARY SERVICE.

JOHN MARSHALL was not yet twenty years of age when he enrolled himself in a volunteer company, which had been formed mainly by his efforts. His attention seems to have been wholly given to perfecting himself in the necessary drill and equipment for efficient military service in the field. The zeal and ardor of the young soldier, and the boldness and spirit with which he inspired others at this period, are well represented to us in a graphic account by a kinsman who was an eye-witness of Marshall's first appearance in the rôle of military leader in his own county.

" It was in May, 1775. He was then a youth of nineteen. The muster-field was some twenty miles distant from the court-house, and in a section of the country peopled by tillers of the earth. Rumors of the occurrences near Boston had circulated, with the effect of alarm and agitation, but without the means of ascertaining the truth, for not a newspaper was printed nearer than Williamsburg, nor was one taken within the bounds of the militia company, though large. The captain had called the company together, and was expected to attend, but did not. John Marshall had been appointed lieutenant in it. Soon after Lieutenant Marshall's appearance on the ground, those who knew him clustered about him to greet him, others from curiosity and to hear the news.

He proceeded to inform the company that the captain would not be there, and that he had been appointed lieutenant instead of a better; that he had come to meet them as fellow-soldiers, who were likely to be called on to defend their country and their own rights and liberties, invaded by the British; that there had been a battle at Lexington, in Massachusetts, between the British and Americans, in which the Americans were victorious, but that more fighting was expected; that soldiers were called for, and that it was time to brighten up their fire-arms and learn to use them in the field; and that if they would fall into a single line, he would show them the new manual exercise, for which purpose he had brought his gun, — bringing it up to his shoulder. The sergeants put the men in line, and their fugleman presented himself in front to the right.

" His figure I have now before me. He was about six feet high, straight, and rather slender, of dark complexion, showing little if any rosy red, yet good health, the outline of the face nearly a circle, and within that eyes dark to blackness, strong and penetrating, beaming with intelligence and good nature; an upright forehead, rather low, was terminated in a horizontal line by a mass of raven black hair of unusual thickness and strength; the features of the face were in harmony with this outline, and the temples fully developed. The result of this combination was interesting and very agreeable. The body and limbs indicated agility rather than strength, in which, however, he was by no means deficient. He wore a purple or plain blue hunting shirt, and trousers of the same material fringed with white; and a round black hat, mounted with the buck's tail for a cockade, crowned the figure and the man. He went through the manual exercise, by word and motion, deliberately pronounced and performed in the presence of the company, before he required the men to imitate him; and then proceeded to exercise them with the most perfect temper. Never did man possess a temper more happy, or, if otherwise, more subdued and better disciplined.

"After a few lessons the company were dismissed, and informed that if they wished to hear more about the war, and would form a circle around him, he would tell them what he understood about it. The circle was formed, and he addressed the company for something like an hour. I remember, for I was near him, that he spoke at the close of his speech of the minute battalion about to be raised, and said he was going into it and expected to be joined by many of his hearers. He then challenged an acquaintance to a game of quoits, and they closed the day with foot races and other athletic exercises, at which there was no betting. He had walked ten miles to the muster-field, and returned the same distance on foot to his father's house at Oak Hill, where he arrived a little after sunset." [1]

When news was received of the battle of Lexington, and then of the march of Patrick Henry upon Williamsburg, the colonial capital of Virginia, young Marshall addressed his company in eloquent terms, urging them to prepare for every emergency, and be ready to march to the front at a moment's warning. Lord Dunmore, the Governor, had caused some powder to be seized by night from the magazine belonging to the colony at Williamsburg, and conveyed on board an armed schooner then lying in James River. Patrick Henry immediately assembled an independent company, and with characteristic boldness marched upon the capital to recapture the powder by force. He was, however, met on the way by a messenger from the Governor, who paid the full value of it in money; whereupon Henry and his party returned. Dunmore, having fortified his " palace," issued a proclamation declaring all armed forces in the colony to be rebels. About the same time letters from Dunmore to England were intercepted, which, being filled with misrepresentations, greatly incensed the people. Thus situated, his lordship

---

[1] *Eulogy on John Marshall,* by Horace Binney, pp. 22-24.

became apprehensive of personal danger, abandoned his government, and went on board a man-of-war then lying in James River, and which, having received him, dropped down to Norfolk. About the same time Governor Martin, of North Carolina, took refuge on board a national ship in Cape Fear River, and in South Carolina Lord William Campbell also abandoned his government and retired.

The occurrences to the northward, the hostile attitude of parties at home, and the liability and expectation of being called into immediate service, induced the volunteers of Culpeper, Orange, and Fauquier counties to constitute themselves a regiment of minutemen. This was doubtless the organization to which young Marshall referred, in his address to the militia, as about to be formed. They were the first minute-men raised in Virginia, and numbered about three hundred and fifty. Lawrence Taliaferro was chosen their colonel, Edward Stevens, lieutenant-colonel, and Thomas Marshall, major. The future Chief Justice himself received the appointment of first lieutenant in one of the companies of the same regiment.

These were the citizen soldiery who, John Randolph said in the Senate of the United States, in one of his rambling speeches, " were raised in a minute, armed in a minute, marched in a minute, fought in a minute, and vanquished in a minute." Certainly their appearance was calculated to strike terror into the hearts of the enemy. They were dressed in green hunting shirts, "home-spun, home-woven, and home-made," with the words " *Liberty or Death* " in large white letters on their bosoms. Their banner displayed a coiled rattlesnake, with the motto, " *Don't tread on me.*" They wore in their hats buck-tails, and in their belts tomahawks and scalping-knives. Their savage and warlike appearance excited the terror of the inhabitants as they marched through the country to Williamsburg. Lord Dunmore told his troops before the action at the Great Bridge, which we shall presently describe, that if they fell into the hands of the *shirt-men* they would be scalped; an apprehension, it is said, which induced several of them to prefer death to captivity. To the honor of the *shirt-men*, however, it should be observed that they treated the British prisoners with great kindness — a kindness which was felt and gratefully acknowledged.

Early in June Lord Dunmore, then at Norfolk and still apprehensive for his personal safety, fled on board of a man-of-war. With the British shipping off the coast of Virginia at

his command, he possessed the means of annoy-
ing the Virginians, though without being able
to strike any effective blow. Through the
autumn of 1775 both parties were kept on the
alert, but nothing very serious occurred. At
length, on November 7, Dunmore proclaimed
martial law, denounced as traitors all who were
capable of bearing arms and did not resort to
his majesty's standard, and offered freedom to
all slaves, belonging to rebels, who would join
his majesty's troops. He set up his standard
in Norfolk and Princess Anne counties, pre-
scribed an oath of allegiance, and received a
considerable accession to his force from the
loyalists.

The Virginians had collected provisions for
their troops, which were stored at Suffolk, eighteen miles southwest of Norfolk. To seize these
provisions was an object of great importance
to Lord Dunmore, and to prevent the seizure
was an object of not less moment to the Virginia
troops. The provisional government perceived
clearly the danger of allowing Lord Dunmore
to maintain his foothold at Norfolk, and orders
were issued immediately to Colonel Woodford to
proceed with a detachment of his minute-men,
including Marshall's company, to protect the
supplies at Suffolk, and to drive the enemy
from Norfolk. The opposing forces confronted

each other at the Great Bridge, as it was called, built over a branch of the Elizabeth River, and lying about twelve miles from Norfolk by the only practicable road to Suffolk. Dunmore, apprised of Woodford's movements, selected a strong position on the eastern side of the bridge, and erected a stockade-fort, which was supplied with many pieces of artillery. The approach to the bridge was commanded by his cannon, which were trained upon the causeway over which the Americans must pass. The *morale* of Dunmore's troops, however, was not equal to his entrenchments. They consisted of two hundred regulars, a corps of Norfolk loyalists, and an undisciplined mob of every class and color. Woodford wisely threw up a breastwork at his end of the causeway, and neither party seemed disposed to begin the attack, several days having elapsed without any serious assault on either side. The Virginia troops were much superior to the enemy in number and character, though for the most part unaccustomed to warfare ; yet being young men of character and full of enthusiasm, they were quite ready for the conflict.

Lieutenant Marshall had now his first experience of war, and in the action which followed he is said to have borne an honorable part, contributing largely by his skill and valor, and by the steadiness of his company's fire, to the success of the day.

Colonel Woodford, perceiving that the enemy were reluctant to begin the attack, resorted to stratagem to induce them to do so. An intelligent servant of Major Marshall's, whose fidelity could be relied on, instructed beforehand as to his story, deserted to the enemy and carried a report that the troops at the other end of the causeway did not exceed three hundred *shirtmen.* Dunmore, deceived by this report, determined to advance to the attack, and dispatched his regulars, with about three hundred blacks and loyalists, to drive the Virginians from their position. The attack was led, on December 9, by Captain Fordyce, a brave and accomplished officer. The assailants were exposed, as they advanced, to the galling fire of the Virginia troops, who were protected by their breastwork. The effect was overpowering. Not more than twenty or thirty minutes were consumed in the action, and then the British, with a heavy loss, were totally routed. They abandoned their entrenchments, spiked their cannon, and fled precipitately to their ships at Norfolk. The Virginians pursued them into Norfolk, and here Marshall remained with his corps, until the town was bombarded and burned by the British men-of-war on January

2

1. Then, there being no longer occasion for
his services there, his company returned to
their homes in Fauquier.

They were not permitted, however, to remain
long inactive, but were reorganized and became
a part of the eleventh regiment of Virginia
troops. They were then ordered to join the
army of Washington in New Jersey, which was
falling back slowly before the British troops
commanded by Sir William Howe, who was
soon after succeeded by Sir Henry Clinton.
The American army, notwithstanding its suc-
cesses at Trenton and Princeton, was in a
wretched condition, both as to numbers and
matériel. Washington's letters describing its
wants and necessities, and urging relief from
the authorities, were so touching as to draw
tears from those who read them. In view of
the actual state of affairs, he wrote, " nothing
but a good face and false appearances have
enabled us to deceive the enemy concerning
our strength." When Marshall joined the army
of Washington in the Jerseys, during this period of profound gloom, patient endurance of
suffering formed the highest quality of the soldier.

On the opening of the campaign in May,
1777, Lieutenant Marshall was promoted to a
captaincy, but in a position thus subordinate

he had slender opportunities to distinguish himself or to attract the eye of his superiors. It can only be said that he omitted no opportunity to engage in the most active service that offered. He was personally engaged, with his command, in the battles of Iron Hill, Brandywine, Germantown, and Monmouth, where the corps to which he was attached underwent many hardships and performed memorable service.

On December 19, Washington with his exhausted troops went into winter quarters at Valley Forge. The season was one of unusual severity. The cold was extreme, yet the soldiers were often almost naked, without blankets to lie on, and often without shoes, so that their march might sometimes be tracked by the blood from their feet. Their provisions were always scant, and occasionally they were actually destitute; yet they took up their winter quarters within a day's march of the enemy, without other shelter to protect them than the rude huts which they hastily constructed of logs and mud. They submitted to all these hardships and privations without complaint, and were always on the alert against threatened attacks of the enemy, who occupied the city of Philadelphia. Well might Washington say of them that " no history now extant can furnish an instance of an army suffering such uncommon hardships and bearing them with the same patience and fortitude." [1]

Marshall's messmates during this memorable winter were Lieutenant Robert Porterfield, Captain Charles Porterfield, Captain Johnson, and Lieutenant Philip Slaughter. The last-named has left a record of the sufferings they endured from lack of food and clothes. He relates that his own supply of linen was reduced to one shirt, and that, while having this washed, he wrapped himself in a blanket. Most of the officers gave all their clothing, except what they were actually wearing, to their almost naked soldiers. Slaughter had wristbands and a collar made from the bosom of his shirt to complete his uniform for parade. Many of the officers were even more scantily supplied than he, having no under-garment whatever. They all lived in huts, although the snow was up to their knees, and not one soldier in five had a blanket. The country people used to bring them supplies which, though far from inviting, were bought and consumed with great eagerness. The Dutch women might frequently be seen riding into camp seated on great bags, which contained one or two bushels each of apple pies, baked so hard that they could be

---

[1] *Washington's Writings*, vol. v. pp. 321–329.

thrown across the room without being the worse
for it. Yet these were considered a delicacy and
were much enjoyed. Washington every day invited the officers, in rotation, to dine with him
at his private table, but these invitations were
usually declined by reason of the lack of de-
cent clothing to appear in. Slaughter, being in
a state of comparative affluence, often went in
place of the others, in order, as he said, that his
regiment might be represented.

Of Marshall, Slaughter says : —

"He was the best - tempered man I ever knew.
During his sufferings at Valley Forge nothing dis-
couraged, nothing disturbed him. If he had only
bread to eat, it was just as well; if only meat, it
made no difference. If any of the officers mur-
mured at their deprivations he would shame them by
good-natured raillery, or encourage them by his own
exuberance of spirits. He was an excellent companion, and idolized by the soldiers and his brother officers, whose gloomy hours were enlivened by his inexhaustible fund of anecdote."

Another account from a contemporary says
that at this time his judicial capacity and fairness were held in such estimation by many of
his brother officers that, in many disputes of a
certain description, he was constantly chosen
arbiter ; and that officers, irritated by difference
and animated by debate, often submitted the

contested points to his judgment, which, given
in writing, and accompanied, as it commonly
was, by sound reasons in support of his decision, obtained general acquiescence. At this
period, besides his field service, he acted as
deputy judge advocate of the army, and thus
came into personal relations with Washington,
securing a confidence and regard of life-long
duration.

On the evacuation of Philadelphia by Sir
Henry Clinton, in June, 1778, the American
force was immediately put in motion with a
view to harass and annoy the retreating army.
Marshall was in the battle of Monmouth, which
ensued, and he remained with his command
throughout the campaign as well as during the
succeeding winter. About this time he was so
fortunate as to be connected with two of the
most brilliant actions that occurred during the
campaign of 1779. He was with Wayne at
the assault on Stony Point, on the night of
June 16; and subsequently with the detachment to cover the retreat of Major Lee, after
his surprise of the enemy's post at Powles's
Hook, on July 19, an enterprise which re-
flected lustre on the American arms.

Toward the close of that year, a part of the
Virginia line was detached and sent to South
Carolina, to coöperate in the defense of that

State ; but it so happened that Marshall was attached to the other part, which remained with
Washington, but whose term of enlistment soon
after expired. He was thus left without any
command, and was ordered with other supernu-
meraries to return to Virginia and take charge
of such men as the State might raise for them,
it being in the contemplation of the General
Assembly to raise a new corps to supply the
place of those whose term of service had thus
come to an end. Accordingly he repaired to
Williamsburg, where the legislature was in session. While the subject was under discussion
in the General Assembly and awaiting its tardy
action, he took advantage of the opportunity
to attend a course of law lectures delivered by
the learned and celebrated Chancellor Wythe,
of William and Mary College ; also the lectures of Bishop Madison, the president of the
college, on natural philosophy. Thus he was
enabled in the ensuing summer to obtain a license to practice law, but his sense of duty to
his country soon drew him back to the army.
The project for raising additional forces in Virginia seems to have failed, and tired of inaction,
he set out alone and on foot to make the long
and wearisome journey to headquarters. On
his arrival in Philadelphia, it is said that his
appearance and outfit were so shabby that the

landlord of the hotel to which he came refused him admittance. He thus resumed his connection with the army; but soon afterward, hearing of the invasion of Virginia by the British troops under General Leslie, in 1780, he again returned thither, and joined the small force under Baron Steuben, who had been left by General Greene (on his way to assume the command of the southern army) for the defense of the State. General Leslie finding, however, that he could not effect a junction with Cornwallis, finally sailed for Charleston. When, subsequently, the State was again invaded by Arnold, Captain Marshall joined the forces collected to oppose him, and continued in service to the latter part of January, 1781, when Arnold had retired discomfited to Portsmouth. There being still a redundancy of officers of the Virginia line, and no additional troops being raised for them to command, he was unwilling to remain longer a supernumerary and resigned his commission.

CHAPTER III.

AT THE BAR.

In 1780–81 Marshall was admitted to the bar and entered on the practice of law in Fauquier County. With his fine abilities, his high character, his family antecedents, and local surroundings in his native county, it is not surprising that his success was assured at once. He was spared the customary ordeal of climbing upward in his profession by the toilsome and rugged road of hard and patient labor. Such was the popular appreciation of his worth that, almost without effort, he secured at once a large clientage, which brought him early prominence and fame at the bar, and a consequently remunerative practice. In fact his clear head and patient industry gave him peculiar qualifications for laboring in the chaos into which the jurisprudence of the State had been plunged by the war. But he was not permitted to pursue without interruption his professional fortunes in provincial courts. The difficulties of the times, especially the putting into safe and harmonious operation the machinery of the new government in the altered condition of affairs, urgently demanded in the public counsels the resources of the wisest heads and the efforts of the best men in the land. He was immediately chosen one of the delegates from Fauquier County to the legislature. It was certainly no small tribute to the character and ability of this young man just come to the bar, and not yet twenty-five years of age, that he should have been selected by the public suffrage to fill a position so conspicuous and responsible. Like Washington, he never sought official station nor public honors, but often shunned them, as we shall see. Nor was he ever a self-announced candidate for any office. All such positions held by him, military, political, and judicial, were given him by the unsolicited confidence of those whose duty it was to bestow them. In his case always "the place sought the man and not the man the place." It is safe to say that, with the exception always of Washington, few of his countrymen, especially in succeeding times, can present a similar record.

It may be supposed that, owing to his long service in the army and the frequent interruption of his law studies on this account, his legal lore could not have been, at this period, either profound or extensive. But what was said of the Virginians by an English historian, who lived among them more than one hundred and fifty years ago, was true especially of John Marshall, namely, " Being naturally of good parts, they neither require nor admire as much learning as they do in Britain." [1]

Marshall rose rapidly at the bar. Once fairly launched in the career of practice, his extraordinary abilities did not fail to make a strong impression on those who witnessed their display. This early success he attributed with native modesty to the friendship of his old comrades in arms. Treated with base ingratitude by the country, the war-worn and poverty-stricken band of the soldiers of the Revolution stood all the more closely together. " They knew," he would say, " that I felt their wrongs and sympathized in their sufferings and had partaken of their labors; and that I vindicated their claims upon their country with a warm and constant earnestness." These veterans all spoke of him in terms of the liveliest praise. Especially the Revolutionary officers of the Virginia line, "now few and faint but fearless still," seemed to idolize him, as an old friend

---

[1] *The Present State of Virginia*, by Hugh Jones, A. M., Chaplain to the Honorable Assembly and lately Minister of Jamestown in Virginia.

and companion who enjoyed their unqualified confidence. They knew his mental qualities and his integrity, and they loved him for the goodness of his heart.

The close of the Revolutionary War was in many respects a fortunate period at which to begin active practice at the bar. So far as the mere amount of business was concerned, a great accession of litigation was the necessary result of the civil and social disruptions wrought by that struggle. The mutations which property had undergone amid the conflicts of a long war, outstanding debts and contracts, and the adjustment of old controversies, became fruitful sources of litigation, and cumbered the dockets of the courts. In the course of a speech in the Virginia Convention of 1788, defending and maintaining the necessity of a federal as well as a state judiciary, Mr. Marshall demanded : " Does not every gentleman here know that the causes in our courts are more numerous than they can decide according to their present construction? Look at the dockets. You will find them crowded with suits, which the life of man will not see determined. If some of these suits be carried to other courts, will it be wrong? They will still have business enough."

Further than this the character of the questions arising, and the condition of the law itself, tended to call forth the highest energies of the profession. Everything seemed new, unsettled, and to be made over afresh. American jurisprudence was as yet unborn. Questions of novel character were constantly arising,— questions to be settled not by authority, but by the light of reason and innate right, and with due reference to the changed condition of political and social affairs. Here the advocate was scarcely either aided or impeded by cases and precedents. In the investigation and argument of such causes he was obliged to rely chiefly on the unassisted powers of his own mind, and to reason from general principles and in the spirit of justice; he could find scant opportunity to adopt as guides the thoughts of others in a different field of investigation. Here the peculiar abilities of Marshall found an appropriate theatre for their employment. It was the legal habit of thought, and the power of construction in sympathy with the spirit of English systems of law, that were needed. This peculiar capacity belonged to Marshall in a rare degree; by the aid of it he afterward shaped the broad outlines of American constitutional law, doing a work more of creation than of learning, and therefore certainly of the highest order. This form of professional work was that which came natural to him. It so happened that the circumstances under which he came to the bar fostered and exercised the tendency. In a different period of judicial development, with different requirements, he would have occupied a less monumental position; but the need of the times and the qualifications of the man were in happy accord.

The system of jurisprudence of which the rules and principles had been laid down in the Virginia Constitution of 1776, with which Marshall was now becoming familiar, had doubtless a strong tendency, in the practice under it, to sharpen the intellect and beget in the bar habits of nice discrimination and close analysis in legal reasoning. The jurisdiction of the courts was wisely distributed among separate tribunals with a view to simplicity, certainty, and economy. Justices of the peace, having original but limited civil and criminal jurisdiction, were appointed by the Governor on the nomination of the county courts. These magistrates formed, when assembled in monthly and quarterly sessions at their court-houses, the county courts, four members making a quorum in all civil, and five in all criminal, causes. These being selected from the gentry of the county were, almost without exception, men of property, of superior intelligence, and high character. They received no compensation for their services, beyond the chance of succession by seniority to the office of high sheriff of the county, a lucrative position of dignity and importance, which was fixed at the term of two years. The circuit and the superior courts of law were of wider jurisdiction, and had fixed pay for the judges. They exercised original jurisdiction in all civil cases, and appellate jurisdiction from the county courts on points of law in all criminal cases, except in the trial of slaves, in which the county courts were courts of oyer and terminer; all five of the members, however, had to concur in their judgments, otherwise the prisoner was entitled to a discharge. The decisions of the circuit courts were subject to appeal on points of law in criminal causes to the general court, an appellate tribunal of the last resort, composed of a majority of the circuit judges, who met annually at the seat of government to try such causes.

The chancery courts, whose jurisdiction was confined exclusively to equity, were held in certain districts of the State, and from their decrees appeals lay to the supreme court of appeals at Richmond, as the court of last resort.

This judicial system, thus briefly outlined, subject to such modifications as the legislature

had, from time to time, enacted, prevailed in
Virginia from the close of the Revolutionary
War to the year 1829–30, — a period of nearly
fifty years, when a convention was called and
a new constitution framed in the interests of
progress and reform. In the judgment of
many wise and considerate men in Virginia
these departures in the several new constitutions, since enacted, from the wisely adjusted
and nicely balanced system of our Revolutionary fathers in 1776, have not proved happy,
nor promoted the public good.

This court system naturally tended to con-
centre the most important cases and the chief
business of litigation in the new metropolis at
Richmond, and thither accordingly the ablest
provincial lawyers necessarily gravitated. For
in consequence of the extent of territory to be
traversed, and of the slow and expensive mode
of travel at that day to reach the capital, the
country lawyers seldom followed their causes
to the appellate courts at Richmond. The
result was that the more successful country
practitioners soon saw the wisdom of enlarging
their sphere of practice by transferring their
offices to the metropolis. Thus it was that
Marshall, after a practice of only two years at
the bar of Fauquier and in the adjacent courts,
having already established himself in a good

business and acquired a reputation which was further enhanced by his able service in the legislature, removed his office to Richmond, where his increasing business and popularity placed him almost at once at the head of his profession.

It was during his service in the legislature that he was elected by that body a member of the state or executive council; and he was made also a general in the new organization of the state militia under the peace establishment.

At the metropolitan bar of his native State Mr. Marshall was brought into active competition with rivals of distinguished fame, — a bar which boasted at that time the names of Patrick Henry, John Wickham, James Innes, Alexander Campbell, Benjamin Botts, and Edmund Randolph. He took rank at once with these as equals, and soon became known and recognized as chief among them. Yet there was nothing in his appearance, manners, or habits to attract attention or to conciliate the interests of the public. On the contrary, in the eyes of ordinary acquaintances, he seemed destitute of those attributes of person and manner which render men attractive and insure professional employment and preferment. We have some accounts, written at that early day, of his

3

personal appearance and rustic manners, which
are characteristic.

" He was one morning strolling through the streets
of Richmond, attired in a plain linen round-about
and shorts, with his hat under his arm, from which he
was eating cherries, when he stopped in the porch of
the Eagle Hotel, indulged in some little pleasantry
with the landlord, and then passed on. Mr. P., a
gentleman from the country then present, who had a
case coming on before the court of appeals, was
referred by the landlord to Marshall, as the best advocate for him to employ; but the careless, languid
air of the young lawyer had so prejudiced Mr. P. that
he refused to engage him. On entering court, Mr.
P. was a second time referred by the clerk of the
court to Mr. Marshall, and a second time he declined.
At this moment entered Mr. V., a venerable-looking
legal gentleman in a powdered wig and black coat,
whose dignified appearance made such an impression
on Mr. P. that he at once engaged him. In the first
case which came on, Marshall and Mr. V. each addressed the court. The vast inferiority of his
advocate was so apparent that, at the close of the
case, Mr. P. introduced himself to young Marshall,
frankly stated the prejudice which had caused him, in
opposition to advice, to employ Mr. V., that he extremely regretted his error, but knew not how to
remedy it. He had come into the city with one hundred dollars as his lawyer's fee, and had but five left,
which, if Marshall chose, he would cheerfully give

him for assisting in the case. Marshall, pleased with the incident, accepted the offer — not however without passing a sly joke at the *omnipotence* of a powdered wig and black coat." [1]

The qualities of mind, more important than these matters of external appearance, which earned for Mr. Marshall his great reputation as a lawyer and an orator at the bar, are thus graphically delineated by the graceful pen of William Wirt, one of the forensic contemporaries of his later career.

" This extraordinary man," says Mr. Wirt, " without the aid of fancy, without the advantages of person, voice, attitude, gesture, or any of the ornaments of an orator, deserves to be considered as one of the most eloquent men in the world ; if eloquence may be said to consist in the power of seizing the attention with irresistible force, and never permitting it to elude the grasp until the hearer has received the conviction which the speaker intends. Ilis voice is dry and hard ; his attitude, in his most effective orations, was often extremely awkward ; while all his gesture proceeded from his right arm and consisted merely in a perpendicular swing of it from about the elevation of his head to the bar, behind which he was accustomed to stand. As to fancy, if she hold a seat in his mind at all, his gigantic genius tramples with disdain on all her flower-decked plats and blooming parterres. How then, you will

[1] Howe's *Historical Collections*, p. 266.

ask, how is it possible, that such a man can hold the
attention of his audience enchained through even a
speech of ordinary length? I will tell you. He
possesses one original and almost supernatural faculty; the faculty of developing a subject by a single
glance of his mind and detecting at once the very
point on which every controversy depends. No matter what the question; though ten times more knotty
than 'the gnarled oak,' the lightning of heaven is not
more rapid or more resistless than his astonishing
penetration. Nor does the exercise of it seem to
cost him an effort. On the contrary, it is as easy as
vision. I am persuaded that his eyes do not fly over
a landscape and take in its various objects with more
promptitude and facility than his mind embraces and
analyzes the most complex subject.

" Possessing, while at the bar, this intellectual
elevation, which enabled him to look down and comprehend the whole ground at once, he determined
immediately and without difficulty on which side the
question might be most advantageously approached
and assailed. In a bad cause his art consisted in
laying his premises so remotely from the point directly in debate, or else in terms so general and so
specious, that the hearer, seeing no consequence which
could be drawn from them, was just as willing to
admit them as not; but, his premises once admitted,
the demonstration, however distant, followed as certainly, as cogently, as inevitably, as any demonstration in Euclid. All his eloquence consists in the
apparently deep self-conviction and emphatic earnest-

ness of his manner; the correspondent simplicity and
energy of his style; the close and logical connection
of his thoughts; and the easy gradations by which
he opens his lights on the attentive minds of his
hearers. The audience are never permitted to pause
for a moment. There is no stopping to weave gar-
lands of flowers, to hang in festoons around a favorite argument. On the contrary, every sentence is
progressive; every idea sheds new light on the subject; the listener is kept perpetually in that sweetly
pleasurable vibration, with which the mind of man
always receives new truths; the dawn advances with
easy but unremitting pace; the subject opens gradually on the view; until, rising in high relief, in all
its native colors and proportions, the argument is
consummated by the conviction of the delighted
hearer." [1]

It is impracticable, within the limits of this
work, to cite the particular causes in which
Marshall appeared at the bar at this period of
his career; but there was one *cause célèbre*, the
argument of which won for him such extensive
renown that its fame spread throughout the
Union. It was the case of Ware *v.* Hylton,
familiarly known to the profession as involving
the British debt question, — a question which,
arising in a multitude of cases in all the States
at this time, was causing extremely bitter and
excited controversy. It was tried in the Cir-

[1] *The British Spy*, pp. 178-181.

cuit Court of the United States at Richmond,
before Chief Justice Jay, Judge Iredell, of the
United States Circuit Court, and Judge Griffin,
of the United States District Court. Patrick
Henry, John Marshall, Alexander Campbell,
and James Innes, Attorney General of Virginia, appeared for the American debtors; and
Andrew Roland, John Wickham, Stark, and
Baker were of counsel for the English creditors. Attracted by the eminence of the counsel, as well as the large interests affected by the
decision of the court, an intelligent and ex-
pectant audience were brought together in the
court-room. A distinguished English lady,
the Countess of Huntingdon, on her travels in
this country, had tarried in Richmond and was
present during the trial. After hearing the
several speakers, she remarked that " if any
one of them had spoken in Westminster Hall,
he would have been honored with a peerage."

In this trial Patrick Henry made one of the
greatest efforts of his life. Realizing the ability of those with whom he had to cope he
made unusual preparation, and is said to have
shut himself up in his office for three days
without seeing even a member of his family,
his food being handed in to him by a servant.
His argument, which lasted three days, so in-
jured his voice that it never fully recovered its
strength.

It seems well worth while to quote at some length from the report of Marshall's argument, both because of the historical importance of the question at issue and because it will furnish a striking, though inadequate, indication of his habits of thought and manner of reasoning. The point was, whether the act of Virginia, passed during the war, providing that Americans in debt to British creditors might be absolved from their indebtedness by paying the amount into the state treasury, was a bar to the recovery of debts so paid, notwithstanding that the treaty of 1783 provided that creditors on either side should meet with no lawful impediment to the recovery of the full value, in sterling money, of all subsisting *bonâ fide* debts theretofore contracted.

" The case resolves itself," said Mr. Marshall, " into two general propositions. First, that the act of Assembly of Virginia is a bar to the recovery of the debt, independent of the treaty. Secondly, that the treaty does not remove the bar.

" That the act of Assembly of Virginia is a bar to the recovery of the debt introduces two subjects for consideration : —

" First, whether the legislature had power to extinguish the debt? Secondly, whether the legislature had exercised that power?

" First. It has been conceded that independent nations have in general the right of confiscation, and

that Virginia, at the time of passing her law, was
an independent nation. But it is contended that,
from the peculiar circumstances of the war, the citizens of each of the contending nations having been
members of the same government, the general right
of confiscation did not apply, and ought not to be exercised. It is not, however, necessary for the defendant in error to show a parallel case in history, since
it is incumbent on those who wish to impair the sovereignty of Virginia to establish on principle or precedent the justice of their exception. That State
being engaged in a war necessarily possessed the
powers of war; and confiscation is one of those powers, weakening the party against whom it is employed
and strengthening the party that employs it. War,
indeed, is a state of force; and no tribunal can decide
between the belligerent powers. But did not Virginia
hazard as much by the war as if she had never been
a member of the British empire? Did she not hazard more, from the very circumstance of its being a
civil war? It will be allowed that nations have
equal powers; and that America, in her own tribunals at least, must, from the 4th of July, 1776, be
considered as independent a nation as Great Britain.
Then what would have been the situation of American property had Great Britain been triumphant in
the conflict? Sequestration, confiscation, and pro-
scription would have followed in the train of that
event; and why should the confiscation of British
property be deemed less just in the event of the
American triumph? The rights of war clearly exist

between members of the same empire engaged in a
civil war.

" But, suppose a suit had been brought during the
war by a British subject against an American citizen, it could not have been supported ; and if there
was a power to suspend a recovery, there must have
been a power to extinguish the debt. They are, indeed, portions of the same power, emanating from
the same source. The legislative authority of any
country can only be restrained. by its own municipal
constitution. This is a principle that springs from
the very nature of society ; and the judicial authority
can have no right to question the validity of a law,
unless such a jurisdiction is expressly given by the
constitution. It is not necessary to inquire how the
judicial authority should act if the legislature were
evidently to violate any of the laws of God; but
property is the creature of civil society and subject,
in all respects, to the disposition and control of civil
institutions. . . .

" But it is now to be considered whether, if the
legislature of Virginia had the power of confiscation,
they have exercised it ? The third section of the
act of Assembly discharges the debtor; and on the
plain import of the term it may be asked, if he is
discharged how can he remain charged? The expression is, 'he shall be discharged from the debt,'
and yet it is contended he shall remain liable for the
debt. Suppose the law had said that the debtor
should be discharged from the commonwealth, but
not from his creditor, would not the legislature have

betrayed the extremest folly in such a proposition? and what man in his senses would have paid a far-thing into the treasury under such a law? Yet, in violation of the expressions of the act, this is the construction which is now attempted.

" It is likewise contended that the act of Assembly does not amount to a confiscation of the debts paid into the treasury; and that the legislature had no power, as between creditors and debtors, to make a substitution or commutation in the mode of payment. But, what is a confiscation? The substance and not the form is to be regarded. The State had a right either to make the confiscation absolute or to modify it, as she pleased. If she had ordered the debtor to pay the money into the treasury, to be applied to pub-lic uses, would it not have been, in the eye of reason, a perfect confiscation? She had thought proper, how-ever, only to authorize the payment, to exonerate the debtor from his creditor, and to retain the money in the treasury subject to her own discretion as to its future appropriation. As far as the arrangement has been made, it is confiscatory in its nature, and must be binding on the parties, though, in the exercise of her discretion, the State might choose to restore the whole or any part of the money to the original cred-itor. Nor is it sufficient to say that the payment was voluntary in order to defeat the confiscation. A law is the expression of the public will, which, when ex-pressed, is not the less obligatory because it imposes no penalty. . . .

" Having thus, then, established that at the time of

entering into the treaty of 1783, the defendant owed
nothing to the plaintiff, it is next to be inquired
whether that treaty revived the debt in favor of the
plaintiff, and removed the bar to a recovery, which
the law of Virginia had interposed?   The words of
the fourth article of the treaty are, that creditors on
either side shall meet with no lawful impediment to
the recovery of the full value in sterling money of all
bonâ fide debts heretofore contracted.   Now, it may
be asked, who are creditors?   There cannot be a
creditor where there is not a debt; and British debts
were extinguished by the act of confiscation.   The
articles, therefore, must be construed with reference
to those creditors who had *bonâ fide* debts subsisting,
in legal force, at the time of making the treaty; and
the word recovery can have no effect to create a debt,
where none previously existed.   Without discussing
the power of Congress to take away a vested right
by treaty, the fair and rational construction of the instrument itself is sufficient for the defendant's cause.
The words ought surely to be very plain that shall
work so evident a hardship as to compel a man to pay
a debt which he had before extinguished.   The treaty
itself does not point out any particular description of
persons who were to be deemed debtors, and it must
be expounded in relation to the existing state of
things.

"It is not true that the fourth article can have no
meaning, unless it applies to cases like the present.
For instance, there was a law of Virginia which pro-
hibited the recovery of British debts that had not

been paid into the treasury. These were *bonâ fide* subsisting debts; and the prohibition was a legal impediment to the recovery, which the treaty was intended to remove. So likewise in several other States laws have been passed authorizing a discharge of British debts in paper money, or by a tender of property at a valuation, and the treaty was calculated to guard against such impediments to the recovery of the sterling value of those debts. It appears, therefore, that, at the time of making the treaty, the state of things was such that Virginia had exercised her sovereign right of confiscation, and had actually received the money from the debtors to the British. If debts thus paid were within the scope of the fourth article, those who framed the article knew of the payment; and upon every principle of equity and law it ought to be presumed that the recovery, which they contemplated, was intended against the receiving State, not against the paying debtor. Virginia possessing the right of compelling a payment for her own use, the payment to her, upon her requisition, ought to be considered as a payment to the attorney or agent of the British creditor. Nor is such a substitution a novelty in legal proceedings; a foreign attachment is founded upon the same principle. . . .

" This act of Virginia must have been known to the American and British commissioners ; and therefore cannot be repealed without plain and explicit expressions directed to that object. Besides, the public faith ought to be preserved. The public faith was plighted by the act of Virginia ; and, as a revival of the debt in question would be a shameful violation of the faith of the State to her own citizens, the treaty should receive any possible interpretation to avoid so dishonorable and so pernicious a consequence. It is evident that the power of the government to take away a vested right was questionable in the minds of the American commissioners, since they would not exercise that power in restoring confiscated real estate; and confiscated debts or other personal estate must come within the same rule."

William Wirt, in contrasting the powers of John Marshall and Alexander Campbell, writes to a friend in the following terms: —

"From what I have heard of Campbell, I believe that, for mere eloquence, his equal has never been seen in the United States. He and the future Chief Justice went to Philadelphia to argue a certain cause somewhere about 1795 or 1796. They were opposed by Hamilton, Lewis, and others. Campbell played off his Apollonian airs; but they were lost. Marshall spoke, as he always does, to the judgment merely, and for the simple purpose of convincing. Marshall was justly pronounced one of the greatest men of the country. He was followed by crowds, looked upon and courted with every evidence of admiration and respect for the great powers of his mind. Campbell was neglected and slighted, and came home in disgust. Marshall's maxim seems always to have been, 'Aim exclusively at strength;' and from his eminent success I say, if I had my life to go over again, I would practice on his maxim, with the most rigorous severity, until the character of my mind was established." [1]

Any abstract of an argument by a mind so analytical as Marshall's would present an inadequate picture of its power. The most that an historian can hope to effect by any statement of it is to show his habit of resolving every proposition he intended to maintain or to attack into its original elements, and by that rigid analysis to develop its strength or to demonstrate its weakness. This is certainly the simplest, the most direct, and the most successful style of reasoning at the bar. His argument in Ware *v.* Hilton happily illustrates this mode, which the French language expresses better than our own, by the word *approfondir*, — "*to go to the bottom of.*" He was thus accustomed to reduce his arguments to one strong point, which he made the pivot of the controversy, and around which he made all inferior considerations to revolve. Although the final decision of this case was adverse to him, the argument secured him great reputation and widely enlarged the sphere of his practice, which, for several years before his partial withdrawal from the bar in consequence of other and higher employments, exceeded that of any other lawyer in Virginia.

[1] Kennedy's *Wirt*, ii. 83.

So great and widespread was the fame of the bar of Richmond at this time, that it attracted the presence and attention of travelers and foreigners. In a book of travels in the United States, by one of these distinguished visitors, the Duke de Liancourt, a French peer, we get the impression made upon an intelligent foreign observer of men and manners in America at that period. Speaking of Edmund Randolph, the ex-secretary of state, the Duke says : " He has a great practice, and stands in that respect nearly on a par with Mr. J. Marshall, the most esteemed and celebrated counselor of this town. The profession of a lawyer is here, as in every other part of America, one of the most profitable ; but though the employment is here more constant than in Carolina, the practitioner's emoluments are very far from being equally considerable. Mr. Marshall does not, from his practice, derive above four or five thousand dollars per annum, and not even that sum every year." After a more familiar acquaintance with the public men at the capital of Virginia, the same writer says : —

" Mr. J. Marshall, conspicuously eminent as a professor of the law, is beyond all doubt one of those who rank highest in the public opinion at Richmond. He is what is called a Federalist, and perhaps, at times, somewhat warm in support of his opinions, but never exceeding the bounds of propriety, which a man of his goodness and prudence and knowledge is incapable of transgressing. He may be considered as a distinguished character in the United States. His political enemies allow him to possess great talents, but accuse him of ambition. I know not whether the charge be well or ill grounded, or whether that ambition might ever be able to impel him to a dereliction of his principles, — conduct of which I am inclined to disbelieve the possibility on his part. He has already refused several employments under the general government, preferring the income derived from his professional labors (which is more than sufficient for his moderate system of economy) together with a life of tranquil ease in the midst of his family and his friends. Even by his friends he is taxed with some little propensity to indolence, but even if this reproach were well founded he nevertheless displays great superiority in his profession when he applies his mind to business."

On January 3, 1783, Marshall was married to Mary Willis Ambler, a daughter of Jacqueline Ambler, then treasurer of Virginia. On the mother's side she was a descendant of the La Roche Jacquelines of France. He had been attached to this lady before he left the army, but they were not married until about the time of his taking up his residence in Richmond. It proved to be a union which constituted, as he declares, the chief happiness of his life, and which endured in uninterrupted affection and confidence for a period of more than fifty years.

CHAPTER IV.

AT the session of 1782 Mr. Marshall took his seat in the General Assembly of Virginia as a member from the county of Fauquier. He was then twenty-seven years of age, already in the front rank of his profession as a lawyer, but as yet without any experience in political affairs. His stirring, active life in the army, and the constantly increasing demands on his time and energies in the professional career opened to him in the courts, had left him slender opportunity to study the science of government, or even to pursue with constancy a course of general reading. But his native sagacity, aided by his observation and experience in life, especially while serving in the army under Washington, where he had observed the defects of the system established under the Articles of Confederation, and the mischiefs flowing therefrom, had led him to see and recognize the absolute necessity of a central authority in

4

the government, which should be sufficiently strong to assert and sustain itself without awaiting the tardy and uncertain coöperation of an unwieldy constituency, like the States acting separately. With these convictions he naturally attached himself to the party which, while ardently republican, yet advocated a general government strong enough to insure the public safety, and to execute the powers with which it might be clothed, *proprio vigore*, independently of control by the several States. His attachment to such a union as this was warm and sincere, and was fostered by all the circumstances of his early career in life.

The influence of these reflections served in his sober judgment, as he wrote in after years, to chasten and subdue "certain enthusiastic notions with which he was tinctured" in the early Revolutionary era. In a letter to a friend, at that subsequent period, he said: —

"The questions which were perpetually recurring in the state legislatures, and which brought annually into doubt principles which I thought most sacred; which proved that everything was afloat and that we had no safe anchorage ground, gave a high value in my estimation to that article in the constitution which imposes restrictions on the States. I was consequently a determined advocate for its adoption, and became a candidate for the state convention.

"When I recollect the wild and enthusiastic notions with which my political opinions of that day
were tinctured, I am disposed to ascribe my devotion
to the Union, and to a government competent to its
preservation, at least as much to casual circumstances
as to judgment. I had grown up at a time when the
love of the Union, and the resistance to the claims of
Great Britain, were the inseparable inmates of the
same bosom. When patriotism and a strong fellow-
feeling with our fellow-citizens of Boston were iden-
tical, when the maxim, ' United we stand, divided we
fall,' was the maxim of every orthodox American.
And I had imbibed these sentiments so thoroughly
that they constituted a part of my being. I carried
them with me into the army, where I found myself
associated with brave men from different States, who
were risking life and everything valuable in a common cause, believed by all to be most precious, and
where I was in the habit of considering America as
my country and Congress as my government."

Adverting to the hardships the army had endured, he adds: —

" My immediate entrance into the state legislature
opened to my view the causes which had been chiefly
instrumental in augmenting those sufferings ; and the
general tendency of state politics convinced me that
no safe and permanent remedy could be found but in
a more efficient and better organized general government."[1]

---

[1] Story's *Discourse on the Life, etc., of Marshall.*

The legislature convened not long after the surrender of Cornwallis at Yorktown, on the nineteenth day of October, 1781. This was practically the close of the war in Virginia. It was not difficult to see that very grave questions of state and national policy would engage the attention of the General Assembly at such a juncture, and that much of good or evil might flow from its deliberations and from its decisions upon the many social and political problems which so strongly agitated the public mind.

Prominent and very urgent among these problems was the necessity for making immediate provision for the payment of our officers and soldiers, now about to be disbanded, who were destitute, in most cases, of the means of subsistence, while the State was largely in their debt. To devise a prompt and efficient remedy for this pressing need, Mr. Marshall exerted himself to the utmost, but the difficulties growing out of the peculiar condition of the country seemed at the time to be almost insurmountable. Yet he knew well, by personal experience, the hardship and privations which the army had endured in this noble struggle for independence, and he had the cause of his late comrades very near his heart. But it was doubtful how much the most energetic efforts could accomplish in the way of justice or even partial relief for these men. For the condition of the country at that period was indeed deplorable. There was not a dollar in the federal treasury, and the State's exchequer was scarcely better supplied. The army was without pay, provisions, or clothing, simply because there was neither public money nor public credit. The repeated and now almost chronic failures of the States to comply with the *pro rata* requisition of the Congress for supplies had long ago begun to produce most disastrous results. It seemed as though the end had been reached in utter helplessness and bankruptcy.

Such was the sense entertained by Congress of the imminence of the public danger, and such the apprehensions of civil convulsions resulting from these evils, that they dispatched to the Eastern and Southern States a deputation, consisting of John Rutledge, of South Carolina, and George Clymer, of Pennsylvania, two of their own body, to explain in person the condition of affairs, and the danger which menaced the country through the delinquency of those States which remained so grossly backward in meeting the requisitions made by Congress on behalf of the army, for the relief of the public credit, and payment of the debts contracted in prosecuting the war for independence. In the discharge of this duty, the delegates visited Richmond, and were permitted personally to address the General Assembly. As a member of that body, Marshall became an earnest advocate of their mission, and of all the measures which tended to arrest immediate danger, to apply the resources of the State to the discharge of her obligations, to strengthen the federal authority, and to enable it to perform its duty towards the army and the public creditors. But the State of Virginia was at that time so weak and so exhausted by previous drains on her resources, and the confederacy was so feeble and powerless, hampered and even paralyzed by the absurd restrictions on its powers imposed by the Articles of Confederation, that Marshall clearly perceived that the system of voluntary state contributions for the relief of the public necessities was a total failure, and that the only means of reanimating the public life and restoring public credit lay in the creation of a more vigorous, independent, and comprehensive general government. This conviction, first borne in upon him at this time, became thereafter the leading idea of his political creed, to which he adhered with firmness and constancy, but without rancor or bitterness of party feeling, to the end of his life. He thus early cast in his political lot with those who were soon to become consolidated as the Federalist party; and to the same principles he remained unalterably attached to the end of his days. He did not adopt this political creed as a matter of free choice; but his mental characteristics were such that he inevitably fell in with this division of the nation. His natural way of thinking was the Federalist way.

Some time after the close of his service in the legislature, he resigned his seat in the executive council chamber, that he might devote himself more closely to his profession; but the condition of the country and the necessities of the public service would not permit him to remain in the coveted seclusion of private life. At the election in Fauquier, in the spring of 1784, his old friends and constituents in that county again elected him a member of the General Assembly, although he was no longer an actual resident in the county, but only preserved his eligibility there by reason of his retaining a freehold in her soil. Three years later, in 1787, his adopted county of Henrico, where he resided near Richmond, paid him the same tribute of respect and confidence. Subsequently, also, when a convention was called to deliberate on the Constitution of the United States, which had been framed by the general convention of delegates from the whole Union,

the same constituency elected him a member
of that body, to which the new constitution
was to be submitted for ratification or rejec-
tion.

CHAPTER V.

THE election of Mr. Marshall to the Virginia
Convention of 1788, called to ratify or reject
the constitution proposed for the United States,
was a marked tribute to his abilities on the
part of the people of Henrico County, then
comprising the city of Richmond, and was also
striking evidence of his great personal popularity among them. For a decided majority of
them were warmly enlisted in opposition to the
proposed constitution. The Revolution indeed
was over, and peace, with independence, had
been achieved, but the whole country was in a
state of great agitation as well as of profound
depression and exhaustion, after the severe ordeal of the war. The advent of peace seemed
to make more apparent the impoverishment
caused by the war, and to bring unexpected
difficulties and novel anxieties. Industry was
paralyzed; business almost at a stand; the na-

tional finances scarcely existed except so far as debts might be said to constitute them ; those States which had made great sacrifices to pay their quota of contribution to the public service had been driven to the ruinous resort of issuing a paper currency for this purpose and for their own immediate wants ; more than three hundred millions of paper money had been put into circulation by the Continental Congress, bearing on its face a solemn pledge of the faith of the Union for its due payment, which faith had been as notoriously violated. This money had fallen so low in market value that it required one hundred dollars of it to pay one real dollar of indebtedness, and it soon lost even the semblance of any value at all. The little specie that had lingered in the country had been slowly drained from it to pay for absolutely necessary supplies from abroad. Not even the interest on the national debt was met. The army had been disbanded unpaid, and the just claims of those brave men who had won our independence were heard only to be unheeded. Private credit was generally hardly better than public. Agriculture and commerce — those breasts of the State — were dried up, and our artisans were idle and starving.

Under such circumstances the popular murmurs of discontent were deep and loud, and were only restrained from developing into overt acts of intestine strife by the wisdom and moderation of the best men and most influential patriots of the land. As Judge Story justly remarks in his striking picture of these times: " In short, we seemed to have escaped from the parent country only to sink into a more galling domestic bondage. Our very safety was felt to be mainly dependent upon the jealousy or forbearance of foreign governments." A further aggravation of these evils arose from the utter hopelessness of any remedy or redress by the then existing national government. That government, created by the Articles of Confederation, was a temporary expedient to unite the States in the maintenance of the war, and was not at all adapted to the changed condition of affairs when that struggle was over. It possessed scarcely any of the attributes of an efficient administration, and was in fact a government only in name.

In view of such known and demonstrated imbecility, it seems strange at this day that the Articles of Confederation should have found any advocates or apologists of their longer endurance. Nevertheless, the fact remains to surprise us that a large party in Virginia and other Southern States, in some of them even a majority of the people, comprising men of in-

telligence and influence who had borne prominent and distinguished parts in the late war of
independence, at the first presentation of the
subject arrayed itself in open opposition to any
effort to found a new and more efficient government. These persons insisted that the States
were fully competent to administer national
affairs under the existing articles, with some
unimportant amendments. It is easy to believe, from what we have already learned of
his antecedents, that Mr. Marshall was not
of this party. On the contrary, he lost no fit
opportunity to declare his open advocacy of
the call for a general convention of the States,
and subsequently to make known his warm
support of the constitution which that convention framed. He took this position from an
honest and intrepid conviction that it was wise
and right, and without any calculation or consideration of the consequences, in the event of
its unpopularity with the voters. As it was almost certain that in Henrico County, where he
then resided, a strong majority were opposed
to the ratification of the constitution, he had
little expectation of being a member of the
convention. Ardently desirous that the constitution should be adopted, he had taken an
active part in the discussion of its necessity in
the General Assembly of Virginia, and before

the people in those popular meetings which
had been held in all parts of the country to
consider and discuss its provisions. When it
was known that a majority of the people of
Henrico were opposed to it, he was assured
that if he would become a candidate and would
pledge himself to vote against it, all opposition
to him would be withdrawn ; otherwise, he was
forewarned that his election would be strenuously contested. He did not hesitate a moment. He discarded the unworthy proposition,
and proclaimed his firm determination to vote
for the constitution if he should get the chance.
Under these unpromising circumstances he was
pressed into the canvass for a seat in the convention, and it was matter of astonishment to
himself and his most sanguine friends when the
result of the polling showed his triumphant
election by a handsome majority. He said
afterward: "In the course of the session of
1788, the increasing efforts of the enemies of
the constitution made a deep impression ; and
before its close a great majority showed a decided hostility to it. I took an active part in
the debates on this question, and was uniform
in the support of the proposed constitution."

Apparently this election of a representative
by a constituency opposed to his well-known
views was the extraordinary result of his per-

sonal popularity. Very popular he certainly
was, so that perhaps no man in Virginia was
more so, and he continued to enjoy the same
favor throughout his long and useful life. He
was eminently fitted by his character and temper to secure without solicitation, and to retain
without artifice, the public esteem and the personal confidence and friendship of all who
knew him. His placid and genial disposition,
his singular modesty, his generous heart, his
kindly and unpretentious manners, the scrupu-
lous respect he showed for the feelings and
opinions of all men, his freedom from pride
and affectation, from humility to the proud and
from pride towards the humble, his candor,
moderation, and integrity, formed such a character that it might be said of him, as of Na-
thanael of old: " Behold an Israelite indeed, in
whom is no guile." These qualities, united to
a higher intelligence and a larger measure of
wisdom and common sense than fell to the
share of most men, naturally conciliated the
confidence and fixed the regard of his fellow-
men. Though party spirit and the political ex-
citements of the hour strongly tended to swerve
men from their equilibrium and to blind their
judgments, he was able to keep the even tenor
of his way, unperturbed by the tempests of passion or prejudice which raged round him.

In view of the object of its convocation, and of the material which formed the membership of the body, it may be safely said that no deliberative assembly ever met in any State more imposing for character, or more renowned for the moral and intellectual gifts and endowments which adorned it, than this Convention of 1788. It presented the very flower of the best population of the ancient commonwealth. The men of education, wealth, and probity, who had attained the highest rank in their several callings, who were most esteemed for purity of character and the elevation of their social relations, had been chosen. Nearly all of them, of both parties, had been engaged in the war of independence, and had served their country in the field or in the legislative or executive councils of the State. They had come up out of great tribulation through the storms and convulsions of war, and bore honorable scars, attesting the severity and sincerity of their self-consecration to the cause of liberty. They were not likely to undervalue the momentous task before them, in laying the foundations of an entirely new government and establishing the polity of a nation.

The convention met at Richmond on the 2d of June, 1788. The fame of the members who composed it, and the unrivaled eloquence of the speakers who were to take part in the discussion of questions of such magnitude, created a vast expectation in the public mind, and attracted large audiences to the place of meeting. The facile pen of Wirt has preserved to us, in his "Life of Patrick Henry," a graphic picture of the gathering and of its debates. He says : —

"Industry deserted its pursuits, and even dissipation gave up its objects, for the superior enjoyments which were presented by the hall of the convention. Not only the people of the town and neighborhood, but gentlemen from every quarter of the State, were seen thronging to the metropolis and speeding their eager way to the building in which the convention held its meetings. Day after day, from morning till night, the galleries of the house were continually filled with an anxious crowd, who forgot the inconvenience of their situation in the excess of their enjoyment ; and far from giving any interruption to the course of the debate, they increased its interest and solemnity by their silence and attention. No bustle, no motion, no sound was heard among them, save only a slight movement when some new speaker arose whom they were all eager to see as well as to hear, or when some master-stroke of eloquence shot thrilling along their nerves and extorted an involuntary and inarticulate murmur. Day after day was this banquet of the mind and of the heart spread before them with a delicacy and variety which could never cloy."

When we enumerate on the one side, among those who opposed the ratification of the constitution, men of such fame as Patrick Henry, George Mason, and William Grayson, an union of eloquence, learning, and ability unsurpassed and but rarely equaled, and behold in the opposite ranks the venerable Edmund Pendleton (who presided over their deliberations), James Madison, and Edmund Randolph, the Governor of the commonwealth, James Innes, the Attorney General of Virginia, a gentleman of known accomplishments and great eloquence, — "an eloquence," said Patrick Henry, "splendid, magnificent, and sufficient to shake the human mind," — Henry Lee of Westmoreland, George and William Nicholas, and John Marshall, then but thirty-three years of age, yet well known to fame, it is not surprising that the public mind of Virginia was shaken to its centre by this conflict of the giants among her sons.

As Mr. Marshall, although he had deeply pondered the great questions presented for consideration and debate, was always more willing to listen than to speak, and as he recognized and admitted the greater experience in public affairs, and the excellent abilities of the leaders on his side, he was not anxious himself to descend into the arena and personally to contend for the laurels of victory. When he did speak,

5

however, during the twenty-five day discuse session, he directed his reply chiefl;ated r. Henry's speeches, rightly judging hind ave the great leader of his party, and conclingg that, if this Coryphæus of the opposition ire answered, all other assailants of the conari-tion were silenced.

We shall lay before the reader, gleaned frm the official report of the debates, some exan-ples, taken from Marshall's speeches, of his lgical methods in argument. It would be desr-able to give some satisfactory sketch of his stye and manner when fairly launched in debate, bit all accounts concur that it was so peculiar as to make description difficult if not impracticabl. All agree, however, that it was very effectiv. He was in all respects a contrast to Mr. Henr, whose oratorical abilities were almost unrivalec. Henry was full of fire, passion, and impetuosity, he was by no means devoid of the power of vigorous conception and clear expression, but his style and manner, especially in his exor-dium, were by no means prepossessing or inspir-ing. A clever writer,[1] speaking of these times, thus describes Mr. Marshall as a speaker: —

" So great a mind, perhaps, like large bodies in the'

---

[1] *Sketches and Essays of Public Characters*, by Francis W. Gilmer.

physical world, is with difficulty set in motion. That this is the case with Mr. Marshall is manifest from his mode of entering on an argument, both in conversation and in public debate. It is difficult to rouse his faculties. He begins with reluctance, hesitation, and vacancy of eye. Presently his articulation becomes less broken, his eye more fixed, until finally his voice is full, clear, and rapid, his manner bold, and his whole face lighted up with mingled fires of genius and passion, and he pours forth the unbroken stream of eloquence in a current, deep, majestic, smooth, and strong. He reminds one of some great bird, which flounders on the earth for a while before it acquires impetus to sustain its soaring flight."

The debates in the convention took a wide and discursive range, but Mr. Marshall was averse, from habit, to general disquisition and logical platitudes. Preferring directness and concentration in reasoning, he selected for his own discussion three features in the proposed constitution, with which he was best acquainted and which its opponents deemed most vulnerable. These were, first, the power granted to Congress to lay taxes for the support of the general government, without relegating that duty to the States. Second, the power given to the President to call out the militia. Third, the judicial power conferred on the federal government. These had been strongly denounced as destructive to the rights and even

the existence of the States. On these several
points he spoke with much earnestness and
force. After a brief general survey of the principles of true government, and after pointing
out that the real issue involved in these debates was a choice between despotism and democracy, he pursues the inquiry as to the safety
of conferring power on Congress to raise money
by taxation, to enable it to perform its func-
tions, in the following terms : —

"I conceive that the object of the discussion now
before us is, whether democracy or despotism be most
eligible. I am sure that those who framed the system submitted to our investigation, and those who
now support it, intend the establishment and security
of the former. The supporters of the constitution
claim the title of being firm friends of the liberty
and the rights of mankind. They say that they
consider it as the best means of protecting liberty.
We, sir, idolize democracy. Those who oppose it
have bestowed eulogiums on monarchy. We prefer
this system to any monarchy, because we are convinced that it has a greater tendency to secure our
liberty and promote our happiness. We admire it
because we think it a well-regulated democracy. It
is recommended to the good people of this country;
they are through us to declare whether it be such a
plan of government as will establish and secure their
freedom.

"Permit me to attend to what the honorable gentle-

man [Patrick Henry] has said. He has expatiated
on the necessity of a due attention to certain maxims;
to certain fundamental principles, from which a great
people ought never to depart. I concur with him
in the propriety of the observance of such maxims.
They are necessary in any government, but more
essential to a democracy than to any other. What
are the favorite maxims of democracy? A strict
observance of justice and public faith, and a steady
adherence to virtue. These, sir, are the principles
of a good government. No mischief, no misfortune,
ought to deter us from a strict observance of justice
and public faith.

"Would to Heaven that these principles had been
observed under the present government! Had
this been the case, the friends of liberty would not
be so willing now to part with it. Can we boast
that our government is founded on these maxims?
Can we pretend to the enjoyment of political freedom or security, when we are told that a man has
been, by an act of Assembly, struck out of existence
without trial by jury, without examination, without
being confronted by his accusers and witnesses, without the benefits of the law of the land? Where is
our safety when we are told that this act was justifi-
able, because the person was not a Socrates? What
has become of the worthy member's maxims? Is
this one of them? Shall it be a maxim that a man
shall be deprived of his life without the benefit of
law? Shall such a deprivation of life be justified by
answering that the man's life was not taken *secun*

dum artem, because he was a bad man?[1] Shall it be
a maxim that government ought not to be empowered
to protect virtue ? He says we wish to have a strong,

[1] This reference is to the case of Josiah Phillips, which
Governor Randolph had adduced as an instance of flagrant
departure from national principles, as well as a violation of the
Constitution of Virginia. Randolph had thus stated the facts
of the case : " From mere reliance on general reports a gentleman in the House of Delegates informed the house that a
certain man (Phillips) had committed several crimes, and was
running at large, perpetrating other crimes. He therefore
moved for leave to attaint him. He obtained that leave instantly; no sooner did he obtain it than he drew from his
pocket a bill ready written for that effect; it was read three
times in one day, and carried to the Senate. I will not say
that it passed the same day through the Senate ; but he was
attainted very speedily and precipitately, without any proof
better than vague reports. Without being confronted with
his accusers and witnesses, without the privilege of calling
for evidence in his behalf, he was sentenced to death and was
afterwards actually executed. Was this arbitrary deprivation
of life, the dearest gift of God to man, consistent with the
genius of a republican government ? Is this compatible with
the spirit of freedom ? This, sir, has made the deepest impression on my heart, and I cannot contemplate it without
horror." Elliott's *Debates*, vol. iii. p. 66.

Patrick Henry thus replied: " The honorable gentleman
has given you an elaborate account of what he judges tyrannical legislation, and an *ex post facto* law, in the case of Josiah
Phillips. He has misrepresented the facts. That man was
not executed by a tyrannical stroke of power. Nor was he a
Socrates. He was a fugitive murderer and an outlaw ; a man
who commanded an infamous banditti. And, at a time when
the war was at the most perilous stage, he committed the most
cruel and shocking barbarities. He was an enemy to the human
name. Those who declare war against the human race may be

energetic, powerful government. We contend for a well-regulated democracy. He insinuates that the power of the government has been enlarged by the convention, and that we may apprehend it will be enlarged by others. The convention did not, in fact, assume any power. They have proposed to our consideration a scheme of government, which they thought advisable. We are not bound to adopt it, if we disapprove of it. Had not every individual in this community a right to tender that scheme which he thought most conducive to the welfare of his

struck out of existence as soon as they are apprehended. He was not executed according to those beautiful legal ceremonies which are pointed out by the laws in criminal cases. The enormity of his crimes did not entitle him to it. I am truly a friend to legal forms and methods; but, sir, in this case, the occasion warranted the measure. A pirate, an outlaw, or a common enemy to all mankind, may be put to death at any time. It is justified by the laws of nature and nations." *Ibid.* p. 140.

When this act of attainder passed, Henry was the Governor of Virginia and Jefferson a member of the Assembly. Randolph, who had been hard pressed by Henry in debate, and arraigned for inconsistency in now supporting the constitution when, as a member of the federal convention, he had refused to sign it, brought forward the case of Phillips as a means of retaliation. But Jefferson says that Phillips was not executed under the act of attainder; that he was indicted at common law for either robbery or murder; was regularly tried, convicted, and executed. No use, he says, was ever made of the act of attainder. Governor Randolph acted for the Commonwealth in the prosecution, he being, at that time, Attorney General. Jefferson supposes that there must have been some mistake in the report of Randolph's statement of the case in the convention, as well as in Henry's reply.

See Jefferson's *Works*, vol. vi. pp. 369–440.

country? Have not several gentlemen already demonstrated that the convention did not exceed its
powers? But the Congress have the power of making bad laws, it seems. The Senate with the President, he informs us, may make a treaty which shall
be disadvantageous to us; and that, if they be not
good men, it will not be a good constitution. I shall
ask the worthy member only, if the people at large,
and they alone, ought to make laws and treaties?
Has any man this in contemplation? You cannot
exercise the powers of government personally yourselves. You must trust to agents. If so, will you
dispute giving them the power of acting for you,
from an existing possibility that they may abuse it?
As long as it is impossible for you to transact your
business in person, if you repose no confidence in
delegates, because there is a possibility of their abus-
ing it, you can have no government; for the power
of doing good is inseparable from that of doing evil.

" Let me pay attention to the observation of the
gentleman who was last up [Mr. Monroe], that the
power of taxation ought not to be given to Congress.
This subject requires the undivided attention of this
house. This power I think essentially necessary;
for without it there will be no efficiency in the government. We have had a sufficient demonstration of
the vanity of depending on requisitions. How, then,
can the general government exist without this power?
The possibility of its being abused is urged as an
argument against its expediency. To very little
purpose did Virginia discover the defects in the old

system; to little purpose indeed did she propose improvements; and to no purpose is this plan constructed for the promotion of our happiness, if we refuse it now because it is possible it may be abused. The confederation has nominal powers, but no means to carry them into effect. If a system of government were devised by more than human intelligence it would not be effectual if the means were not adequate to the power. All delegated powers are liable to be abused. Arguments drawn from this source go in direct opposition to all government, and in recommendation of anarchy. The friends of the constitution are as tenacious of liberty as its enemies. They wish to give no power that will endanger it. They wish to give the government powers to secure and protect it. Our inquiry here must be, whether the power of taxation be necessary to perform the objects of the constitution, and whether it be safe, and as well guarded as human wisdom can do it. What are the objects of the national government? To protect the United States and to promote the general welfare. Protection in time of war is one of its primal objects. Until mankind shall cease to have avarice and ambition, wars shall arise. There must be men and money to protect us. How are armies to be raised? Must we not have money for that purpose? But the honorable gentleman says that we need not be afraid of war. Look at history, which has been so often quoted. Look at the great volume of human nature. They will both tell you that a defenseless country cannot be secure. The

nature of man forbids us to conclude that we are in
no danger from war. The passions of men stimulate
them to avail themselves of the weakness of others.
The powers of Europe are jealous of us. It is our
interest to watch their conduct, and guard against
them. They must be pleased with our disunion. If
we invite them, by our weakness, to attack us, will
they not do it? If we add debility to our present
situation, a partition of America may take place. It
is then necessary to give the government that power,
in time of peace, which the necessity of war will render indispensable, or else we shall be attacked unpre-
pared. The experience of the world, a knowledge
of human nature, and our own particular experience,
will confirm this truth. When danger shall come
upon us, may we not do what we were on the point
of doing once already, that is, appoint a dictator?
. . . We may now regulate and frame a plan that
will enable us to repel attacks. and render a recur-
rence to dangerous expedients unnecessary. If we
are prepared to defend ourselves, there will be little
inducement to attack us. But if we defer giving
the necessary power to the general government till
the moment of danger arrives, we shall give it then
and with an *unsparing hand.*

"I defy you to produce a single instance where
requisitions on several individual States, composing
a confederacy, have been honestly complied with.
Did gentlemen expect to see such punctuality complied with in America? If they did, our own experience shows the contrary." . . . "A bare sense of

duty or a regard to propriety is too feeble to induce men to comply with obligations. We deceive ourselves, if we expect any efficacy from these. If requisitions will not avail, the government must have the sinews of war some other way. Requisitions cannot be effectual. They will be productive of delay, and will ultimately be inefficient. By direct taxation the necessities of the government will be supplied in a peaceable manner, without irritating the minds of the people. But requisitions cannot be rendered efficient without a civil war, without great expense of money and the blood of our citizens."

" Is the system so organized as to make taxation dangerous? . . . I conceive its organization to be sufficiently satisfactory to the warmest friend of freedom. No tax can be laid without the consent of the House of Representatives. If there be no impropriety in the mode of electing the representatives, can any danger be apprehended? They are elected by those who can elect representatives in the state legislature. How can the votes of the electors be influenced? By nothing but the character and conduct of the men they vote for."

" If they are to be chosen for their wisdom, virtue, and integrity, what inducement have they to infringe on our freedom? We are told that they may abuse their power. Are there strong motives to prompt them to abuse it? Will not such abuse militate against their own interest? Will not they and their friends feel the effects of iniquitous measures? Does the representative remain in office for life? Does

he transmit his title of representative to his son?
Is he secured from the burdens imposed on the community? To procure their reëlection it will be
necessary for them to confer with the people at large
and convince them that the taxes laid are for their
good. If I am able to judge on the subject, the
power of taxation now before us is wisely conceded,
and the representatives wisely elected."

"The extent of the country is urged as another
objection, as being too great for a republican government. This objection has been handed from author
to author, and has been certainly misunderstood and
misapplied. To what does it owe its source? To
observations and criticisms on governments where
representations did not exist. As to the legislative
power, was it ever supposed inadequate to any extent? Extent of country may render it difficult to
execute the laws, but not to legislate. Extent of
country does not extend the power. What will be
sufficiently energetic and operative in a small territory will be feeble when extended over a wide-
extended country. The gentleman tells us there are
no checks in this plan. What has become of his
enthusiastic eulogium on the American spirit? We
should find a check and control, when oppressed, from
that source. In this country there is no exclusive
personal stock of interest. The interest of the community is blended and inseparably connected with
that of the individual. When he promotes his own,
he promotes that of the community. When we consult the common good, we consult our own. When

he desires such checks as these, he will find them abundantly here. They are the best checks. What has become of his eulogium on the Virginia Constitution? Do the checks in this plan appear less excellent than those of the Constitution of Virginia? If the checks in the constitution be compared to the checks in the Virginia Constitution, he will find the better security in the former."

"The worthy member [Patrick Henry] has concluded his observations by many eulogiums on the British Constitution. It matters not to us whether it be a wise one or not. I think that, for America at least, the government on your table is very much superior to it. I ask you if your House of Representatives would be better than it is if a hundredth part of the people were to elect a majority of them? If your Senators were for life, would they be more agreeable to you? If your President were not accountable to you for his conduct, — if it were a constitutional maxim, that he could do no wrong, — would you be safer than you are now? If you can answer Yes to these questions, then adopt the British Constitution. If not, then, good as that government may be, this is better.

"The worthy gentleman who was last up [Monroe] said the confederacies of ancient and modern times were not similar to ours, and that consequently reasons which applied against them could not be urged against it. Do they not hold out one lesson very useful to us? However unlike in other respects they resemble it in its total inefficacy. They warn us to shun their calamities and to place in our government those necessary powers, the want of which destroyed them. I hope we shall avail ourselves of their misfortunes without experiencing them. There was something peculiar in one observation he made. He said that those who governed the cantons of Switzerland were purchased by foreign powers, which was the cause of their uneasiness and trouble. How does this apply to us? If we adopt such a government as theirs, will it not be subject to the same inconvenience? Will not the same cause produce the same effect? What shall protect us from it? What is our security? He then proceeded to say, the causes of war are removed from us; that we are separated by the sea from the powers of Europe and need not be alarmed. Sir, the sea makes them neighbors to us. Though an immense ocean divides us we may speedily see them with us. What dangers may we not apprehend to our commerce? May not the Algerines seize our vessels? Cannot they, and every other predatory and maritime nation, pillage our ships and destroy our commerce, without subjecting themselves to any inconvenience? He would, he said, give the general government all necessary powers. If anything be necessary, it must be so to call forth the strength of the Union when we may be attacked, or when the general purposes of America require it. The worthy gentleman then proceeded to show that our present exigencies are greater than they will ever be again. Who can penetrate into futurity? How can any man pretend

to say that our future exigencies will be less than
our present? The exigencies of nations have been
generally commensurate to their resources. It would
be the utmost impolicy to trust to a mere possibility
of not being attacked, or obliged to exert the strength
of the community."

" He then told you that your continental government will call forth the virtue and talents of America. This being the case, will they encroach on the
power of the state governments? Will our most
virtuous and able citizens wantonly attempt to destroy the liberty of the people? Will the most virtuous act the most wickedly? I differ in opinion
from the worthy gentleman. I think the virtue and
talents of the members of the general government
will tend to the security, instead of the destruction, of
our liberty. I think that the power of direct taxation is essential to the existence of the general
government, and that it is safe to grant it. If this
power be not necessary and as safe from abuse as any
delegated power can possibly be, then I say that the
plan before us is unnecessary, for it imports not what
system we have unless it have the power of protecting us in time of peace and war."

In respect to the power conferred on the
President to call out the militia, to repel invasion, and to suppress insurrection, etc., Mr.
Marshall asked, in reply to the critics of the
constitution, whether gentlemen were serious
when they asserted that, if the state govern-

ments had power to interfere with the militia, it was only by implication.

"If they were, he asked the committee whether the least attention would not show that they were mistaken. The state governments did not derive their powers from the general government ; but each government derived its powers from the people, and each was to act according to the powers given to it. Would any gentleman deny this? He demanded if powers not given were retained by implication. Could any man say so? Could any man say that this power was not retained by the States, as they had not given it away? For does not a power remain until it is given away ? The state legislatures had power to command and govern their militia be-before, and have it still, undeniably, unless there be something in this constitution that takes it away."
"The truth is, that when power is given to the general legislature, if it was in the state legislature before, both shall exercise it, unless there be an incompatibility in the exercise by one to that by the other, or negative words precluding the state governments from it. But there are no negative words here. It rests, therefore, with the States. To me it appears then unquestionable that the state governments can call forth the militia, in case the constitution should be adopted, in the same manner as they would have done before its adoption.
" When the government is drawn from the people and depending on the people for its continuance, op-

pressive measures will not be attempted, as they will certainly draw on their authors the resentment of those on whom they depend. On this government, thus depending on ourselves for its existence, I will rest my safety, notwithstanding the danger depicted by the honorable gentlemen. I cannot help being surprised that the worthy member thought this power so dangerous. What government is able to protect you in time of war? Will any State depend on its own exertions? The consequence of such dependence and withholding this power from Congress will be that State will fall after State, and be a sacrifice to the want of power in the general government. United we are strong; divided we fall. Will you prevent the general government from drawing the militia of one State to another, when the consequence will be that every State must depend on itself? The enemy, possessing the water, can quickly go from one State to another. No State will spare to another its militia, which it conceives necessary for itself. It requires a superintending power in order to call forth the resources of all to protect all. If this be not done, each State will fall a sacrifice. This system merits the highest applause in this respect. The honorable gentleman said that a general regulation may be made to inflict punishment. Does he imagine that a militia law is to be ingrafted on the scheme of government, so as to render it incapable of being changed? The idea of the worthy member supposes that men renounce their own interests. This would produce general inconveniences through-

6

out the Union, and would be equally opposed by all
the States. But the worthy member fears that in one
part of the Union they will be regulated and disciplined, and in another neglected. This danger is
enhanced by leaving this power to each State, for
some States may attend to their militia, and others
may neglect them. If Congress neglect our militia,
we can arm them ourselves. Cannot Virginia import
arms ? Cannot she put them into the hands of her
militia men ? "

Referring to that clause of the constitution
which related to the federal judicial system,
Mr. Marshall said : —

" Mr. Chairman, this part of the plan before us is
a great improvement on that instrument from which
we are now departing. Here are tribunals appointed
for the decision of controversies which were before
either not at all, or improperly, provided for. That
many benefits will result from this to the members
of the collective society every one confesses. Unless
its organization be defective, and so constructed as to
injure instead of accommodating the convenience of
the people, it merits our approbation. After such a
candid and fair discussion by those gentlemen who
support it, after the very able manner in which
they have investigated and examined it, I conceived
it would be no longer considered as so very defective,
and that those who opposed it would be convinced of
the impropriety of some of their objections. But I
perceive that they still continue the same opposition.

Gentlemen have gone on an idea that the federal courts will not determine the causes which may come before them with the same fairness and impartiality with which other courts decide. What are the reasons of this supposition? Do they draw them from the manner in which the judges are chosen, or the tenure of their office? What is it that makes us trust our judges? Their independence in office, and manner of appointment. Are not the judges of the federal court chosen with as much wisdom as the judges of the state governments? Are they not equally, if not more, independent? If so shall we not conclude that they will decide with equal impartiality and candor? If there be as much wisdom and knowledge in the United States as in a particular State, shall we conclude that that wisdom and knowledge will not be equally exercised in the selection of judges?"

" With respect to its [the federal judiciary's] cognizance, in all cases arising under the constitution and the laws of the United States, he [George Mason] says that, the laws of the United States being paramount to the laws of the particular State, there is no case but what this will extend to. Has the government of the United States power to make laws on every subject? Does he understand it so? Can they make laws affecting the mode of transferring property, or contracts, or claims, between citizens of the same State? Can they go beyond the delegated powers? If they were to make a law not warranted by any of the powers enumerated, it would be considered

by the judges as an infringement of the constitution
which they are to guard. They would not consider
such a law as coming under their jurisdiction. They
would declare it void."

"How disgraceful is it that the state courts cannot
be trusted, says the honorable gentleman. What is
the language of the constitution? Does it take away
their jurisdiction? Is it not necessary that the federal courts should have cognizance of cases arising
under the constitution and laws of the United States?
What is the service or purpose of a judiciary, but to
execute the laws in a peaceable, orderly manner,
without shedding blood, or creating a contest, or
availing yourselves of force? If this be the case,
where can its jurisdiction be more necessary than
here?"

" With respect to disputes between a State and the
citizens of another State, its jurisdiction has been
decried with unusual vehemence. I hope that no
gentleman will think that a State will be called at
the bar of the federal court.[1] Is there no such case
at present? Are there not many cases in which
the legislature of Virginia is a party, and yet the
State is not sued? It is not rational to suppose
that the sovereign power should be dragged before a
court. The intent is to enable States to recover
claims from individuals residing in other States. I

---

[1] This, however, was afterwards done, in the case of Chis-
holm *v.* Georgia. The decision of the court in that case led
to an amendment of the Constitution, forbidding such an exercise of authority.

contend that this construction is warranted by the words. But, say they, there will be partiality in it, if a State cannot be defendant, if an individual cannot proceed to obtain judgment against a State, though he may be sued by a State. It is necessary to be so, and cannot be avoided. I see a difficulty in making a State defendant which does not prevent its being plaintiff. If this be only what cannot be avoided, why object to the system on that account? If an individual has a just claim against any particular State, is it to be presumed that, on application, he will not obtain satisfaction? But how could a State recover any claim from a citizen of another State, without the establishment of these tribunals?

"The honorable member objects to suits being instituted in the federal courts by the citizens of one State against the citizens of another State. Were I to contend that this was unnecessary in all cases, and that the government, without it, would be defective, I should not use my own judgment. But are not the objections to it carried too far? Though it may not, in general, be absolutely necessary, a case may happen, as has been observed, in which a citizen of one State ought to be able to recur to this tribunal to recover a claim from the citizen of another State. What is the evil which this can produce? Will he get more justice there? The independence of the judges forbids it. What has he to get? Justice. Shall we object to this because the citizen of another State can obtain justice without applying to our state courts ? It may be necessary with respect to the laws and regulations of commerce, which Congress may make. It may be necessary in cases of debt, and some other controversies. In claims for land, it is not necessary, but it is not dangerous. In the court of which State will it be instituted ? said the honorable gentleman. It will be instituted in the court of the State where the defendant resides, where the law can come at him, and nowhere else. By the laws of which State will it be determined ? said he. By the laws of the State where the contract was made. According to those laws and those only can it be decided. Is this a novelty ? No ; it is a principle in the jurisprudence of this commonwealth. If a man contracted a debt in the East Indies and it was sued for here, the decision must be consonant to the laws of that country."

These examples of the clearness of Marshall's reasoning serve to show how it was that, at his age, he could win the distinction as a debater which he achieved in the convention. He seemed to impress his opponents very favorably, and though he might not have conquered them by his massive logic, he conciliated their esteem and good-will, which Mr. Henry very handsomely acknowledged. " I have," Henry said, " the highest veneration and respect for the honorable gentleman, and I have experienced his candor on all occasions."

The opponents of the constitution were

largely in the ascendant at the meeting and in the early stages of the convention, but, in the end, its supporters prevailed by a majority of ten votes ; a result which frankness compelled the victors to confess was not due altogether to superior merit in argument, but largely also to the gradual progress of public opinion, and to the persuasive fact that, while the convention was still engaged in grave debate on the subject at Richmond, news was received that nine out of the thirteen States had already given in their adhesion to its adoption — a sufficient number to insure its success.

CHAPTER VI.

AFTER his service in the convention Mr. Marshall again resolved to retire from public life and devote himself to his law business; a course now rendered more necessary by his slender fortune and growing family. But again he was overruled by the earnest appeals of his neighbors to represent them in the ensuing legislature. It had now become manifest that, notwithstanding the adoption of the United States Constitution, the large minority opposed to it were still very active and formidable in their hostility, and were resolved to insure an anti-federal ascendancy in that body. Some of them were willing even to embarrass the new government by any means that might seem likely to defeat its success. Under these circumstances and urged by his constituency, Marshall felt obliged to forego his intended retirement, and thereupon so great were his popularity and influence that he was again triumphantly elected, notwithstanding the fact that an anti-federal majority in the county was known to be against him. He held the position until the spring of 1791.

In the first session of the General Assembly after the adoption of the constitution, he found his party in a minority. The opposition had secured the ascendancy in that body and elected, as the first Senators to Congress from Virginia, Mr. Grayson and Mr. Richard Henry Lee, both of whom had opposed the constitution, in preference to Mr. Madison and Mr. Pendleton, who had so warmly supported it. Such was the virulence of party spirit even at that early day that, notwithstanding the overwhelming personal popularity of Washington, elected without opposition the first President of the United States, all the leading measures of his administration were warmly debated and criticised by the Virginia legislature, with a watchful jealousy.

In so excited a state of popular feeling, Marshall's triumph was a very remarkable instance at once of the magnanimity of many anti-federalists and of his high repute and prestige. But such honors were not so rare in those days as they have since become; similar notable instances, occurring about the same time, will be recalled. The truth is that the mass of the people were singularly fair-minded and anxious to work out for the best the momentous problem before them. Their behavior throughout this crisis was admirably liberal and temperate.

Marshall cherished the highest confidence in the wisdom and patriotism of Washington, and gave his earnest support to all those measures of the national administration which he could approve, although they provoked the animadversion of those who professed to see the horrid Gorgon of consolidation in every measure proposed as a remedy for existing disorders. In the halls of the legislature of Virginia these questions were debated with freedom, earnestness, and ability. In these discussions Mr. Marshall participated with even more than his usual power, defending the administration of Washington with great force of argument, but it is mortifying to reflect with what little effect. The current of party feeling proved too mighty to be resisted. It was an anomalous condition of things that in Virginia at that time Washington, who should have been the most honored and beloved of her sons and benefactors, was opposed in almost every important measure of his administration. The State seemed to set the example in opposition, and to lead the way in disaffection.

Fortunately this unwelcome posture of affairs

at last gave Mr. Marshall his long-coveted opportunity to retire from public life and devote himself, without reserve, to the practice of his profession. In 1792 he positively declined a reëlection to the legislature, and for the succeeding three years devoted himself with energy to his professional duty. The location of his office in Richmond, where the legislature met annually, had enabled him to preserve, in a great degree, his practice in the courts whenever he was not occupied with his legislative duties. Now that he could again give his undivided attention to the law, his business rapidly increased and became handsomely remunerative. It is said that he was employed in nearly every important case in the state and federal courts.

The system of practice was very favorable to the growth and success of eminent counsel at the metropolitan bar. As already stated, it seldom happened that provincial lawyers, however competent and able, owing to the distance, delay, and expense of travel, followed their cases into the appellate courts, which held their sessions in Richmond. Clients who appealed their causes had to resort to counsel in that city, and armed with a copy of the record and a retaining fee of not less than one hundred dollars, they sought the advice of those eminent lawyers who practiced in the courts of appeal.

Mr. Marshall was now so well known throughout the commonwealth, and so highly appreci-
ated in his profession, that he commanded the
largest share of this practice.   The volumes of
Call's and Washington's Reports of Causes argued at that early period in the court of appeals attest the number and importance of the
cases in which he appeared as counsel.   This,
of necessity, extended his professional correspondence with his brethren of the bar throughout the State.   Some of these letters from him
have survived the lapse of time, and furnish oc-
casional glimpses of his friendly geniality and
the fashion of his wit.   For example, here is an
extract from one to his friend Judge Archibald
Stuart : —

"I cannot appear for Donaghoe.   I do not decline
his business from any objection to his *bank.*   To that
I should like very well to have free access, and would
certainly discount *from* it as largely as he would permit ; but I am already fixed by Rankin, and as those
who are once in the bank do not, I am told, readily
get out again, I despair of being ever able to touch
the guineas of Donaghoe.

"Shall we never see you again in Richmond?   I was
very much rejoiced when I heard that you were happily married, but if that amounts to a *ne exeat,* which
is to confine you entirely to your side of the moun-
tain, I shall be selfish enough to regret your good
fortune, and almost to wish you had found some little

crooked rib among the fish and oysters which would once a year drag you into this part of our terraqueous globe. You have forgotten, I believe, the solemn compact we made to take a journey to Philadelphia together this winter, and superintend for a while the proceedings of Congress. I wish very much to see you. I want to observe how much honester men you and I are [than] half one's acquaintance. Seriously, there appears to me every day to be more folly, envy, malice, and damned rascality in the world than there was the day before; and I do verily begin to think that plain, downright honesty and unintriguing integrity will be kicked out of doors.

"We fear, and not without reason, a war. The man does not live who wishes for peace more than I do, but the outrages committed upon us are beyond human bearing. Farewell. Pray heaven we may weather the storm.   Yours,

"J. MARSHALL."

With the known abilities and the avowed political opinions of Mr. Marshall, it was almost impossible for him to withdraw himself entirely from public life. The foreign policy of Washington was not less warmly attacked than his domestic. A fierce and bitter war was pending between France and England, and strong efforts were made by each to draw the new government of the United States into the strife, and to throw its weight into their own scale. Threats were employed by each side to effect this purpose, and France resorted also to blandishments and intrigues. Thomas Jefferson, although the secretary of state in Washington's cabinet, already was, or soon became, the acknowledged leader of the anti-federal party. He hated England, and opposed the idea of an Anglican alliance, while he more furtively but warmly affiliated with France. Early in the year 1793, the French Directory dispatched as minister to the United States the famous M. Genet, who landed in Charleston, South Carolina, and before presenting his credentials to Washington, proceeded at once, with almost incredible presumption, to issue letters of marque and reprisal against British commerce, to fill up officers' blank commissions which he had brought out with him from France, and to dispatch privateers to prey upon British ships at sea, so that the French war ship in which he had made the voyage over had actually captured prizes in American waters before the envoy had had his audience of reception by the President. He remained long in Charleston, and seemed purposely to delay his journey to the seat of government in order to give time for the seeds of sedition, which he was industriously sowing, to germinate, and to commit the people so thoroughly in advance of any governmental action that it would be found impracticable to avoid precipitating hostilities with England. In this the Frenchman counted largely on the feebleness of the administration, and on the strength of the opposition to it. These opponents formed a strong Gallican party, with which it was known that the secretary of state was in sympathy and affiliation.

Genet at length, after much delay, made his slow progress northward, and arriving at Philadelphia, received something of an ovation from the admiring and exultant citizens who sympathized in his mission, and who seemed to find little to condemn in his unparalleled and audacious conduct toward the national government. He was honored with a civic banquet in that city, on which occasion the guests, with wild enthusiasm, sang the "Marseillaise," wore the red liberty cap of French republicanism, and greeted each other by the revolutionary title of "citizen."

Mr. Jefferson, however, had too much sagacity to commit himself to such a policy, or to justify the proceedings of the new minister. His letters in remonstrance against M. Genet's conduct were distinct and emphatic enough to protect their author from the charge of complicity in the seditious and mischievous proceedings of the French emissary. But the acute reader could read between the lines that the

American secretary of state was not devoid of sympathy with the wishes and policy of France, though irritated and indignant at the conduct of the French envoy. From the beginning of his mission this messenger of discord suffered scarcely a day to pass without some new act of aggression, some fresh breach of international law, culminating at length in the arrogance of threatening President Washington, that he, foreigner as he was, himself would publicly appeal from the President to the American people, and would respect the expressions and doings of the executive only when the representatives of the people should have confirmed them. This outrage, and the utter and disgraceful violation of the ordinary courtesies and rights of international intercourse by this French Catiline, induced Washington to demand his immediate recall. This demand was complied with, and thus the obnoxious intruder was banished from the country. The proclamation of neutrality by Washington, in which Mr. Jefferson, as a member of the cabinet, could not avoid concurring, speedily followed.

It challenges our surprise, at this day, that a measure so obviously wise and right as this proclamation of neutrality, and so essential to the vindication of our national dignity and character, should have inflamed anew the opposition to the administration of Washington and increased the animosity of that party; yet such was the case. In public meetings, in legislative proceedings, and in popular discussions, the course of the administration was strongly condemned. It did not accord with Marshall's nature or sense of duty to stand by and tamely submit to such gross injustice to the President and to the country. Acting on what he believed to be just and right and in the best interests of the people, he gave to this and kindred measures of Washington's cabinet his earnest and unwavering support, and readily united with his political friends in the call of a meeting of the citizens of Richmond to consider the state of affairs. Here he offered resolutions approving the President's course, and advocated them in a speech of unusual ability. They were passed by a considerable majority. But his success on this occasion, honorable as it was to himself and gratifying to his friends, was purchased at the usual price of a more vehement and unsparing hostility than ever on the part of his political opponents. Defeated by him in the argument, they now began to assail him with bitter personal reproaches, seeking to undermine his influence and public character by denouncing him as an aristocrat, attached to the British constitution and an enemy to

7

the republican form of government. These unworthy assaults, however, did him little harm. In Richmond, where his purity of character and manner of life were so well known, the ungenerous attacks recoiled on their authors. It was of little use to tell those who knew him that he was a British aristocrat; but the charges traveled, of course, far beyond the circle of his neighbors.

Nor were these feelings of jealousy mitigated by his fearless defense, soon after, of Jay's treaty with England, when that unpopular document came before the United States Senate for ratification. At a public meeting of its opponents, in the city of Richmond, over which the venerable Chancellor Wythe presided, resolutions were adopted denouncing it as insulting to the dignity, injurious to the interest, dangerous to the security, and repugnant to the Constitution of the United States. But at a subsequent meeting of the citizens Mr. Marshall offered resolutions of a contrary character and supported them in an able speech. Besides the expediency of the treaty, its constitutionality also was assailed on the ground that, as the constitution bestowed on Congress the power to " regulate commerce," the executive could not have the right to negotiate a commercial treaty. Marshall addressed himself particu-

larly to this position, and so completely over-
turned it that it was never urged again in
Virginia.

This argument brought Mr. Marshall great
reputation, and first made his name familiar
throughout the country as an expounder of the
constitutional powers of the government. Visiting Philadelphia, a few months after, to argue
the British debt case on appeal to the supreme
court, he became an object of marked attention.

"I then became acquainted," he says, in a letter to
a friend, "with Mr. Cabot, Mr. Ames, Mr. Dexter,
and Mr. Sedgwick, of Massachusetts, Mr. Wadsworth,
of Connecticut, and Mr. King, of New York. I was
delighted with these gentlemen. The particular subject [the British treaty] which introduced me to their
notice was, at that time, so interesting, and a Vir-
ginian with any sort of reputation who supported
the measures of government was such a *rara avis*,
that I was received by them all with a degree of
kindness which I had not anticipated. I was particularly intimate with Mr. Ames, and could scarcely
gain credit with him, when I assured him that the
appropriations [to carry out the treaty] would be
seriously opposed in Congress." [1]

In the spring of 1795, when it became apparent that all these questions would come

.   [1] Story's *Discourse*, p. 40.

up for consideration in the state legislature, and that General Washington's administration would be severely assailed by an unrelenting opposition, Mr. Marshall's friends, anxious to avail themselves of his great services in that crisis, again forced him into a seat in the General Assembly. The circumstances were peculiar and very flattering to him. Party spirit ran high, and so close was the division that it seemed doubtful whether the regular candidate of the Federalists, an intimate personal friend of Mr. Marshall, could be elected. Accordingly a poll was opened for Marshall on the very day of election, while he was engaged in one of the courts, and notwithstanding his resistance and his declaration that his feelings and honor were alike engaged for his friend, he was chosen.

CHAPTER VII.

THE FRENCH MISSION.

1797–1798.

JOHN ADAMS succeeded Washington in the presidency in 1797, and on May 31 of that year nominated as envoys extraordinary and ministers plenipotentiary to France, Charles Cotesworth Pinckney, John Marshall, and Francis Dana. The last named declined the appointment, and Elbridge Gerry took his place.

Marshall accepted this mission with reluctance, but the exigency of affairs was such that he did not feel at liberty to decline it. Having arranged his business at home with dispatch, he was ready to embark in July of the same year. On leaving Richmond for Philadelphia, he was attended for several miles on his journey by a large cavalcade of his fellow-citizens. However assailed he might be by political opponents, these sentiments of personal respect and affection were never wanting on the part of the people. He embarked at Philadelphia for Amsterdam on the 17th of July. President Adams, in a letter to Gerry at that time, says of him : " He is a plain man, very sensible, cautious, guarded, and learned in the law of nations. I think you will be pleased with him."

The ratification of Jay's treaty of amity, commerce, and navigation between the United States and England had been highly offensive to France, not because it contained provisions which were particularly obnoxious to her, but because our ancient ally expected the United States to make no treaty with her enemy. Indeed the exasperation at Paris might well have led to immediate war between the two countries, had not the Directory been preoccupied with European complications, and had they not also hoped that the opposition in Congress would be able to prevent the carrying out of the treaty provisions. But although actual war was thus for the time avoided, a series of hostile acts, both aggressive and retaliatory, was pursued by France, which inflicted much injury on our commerce, and the whole conduct of the French government toward the United States was marked·by intolerable insolence.

In October, 1796, the French government had issued orders directing the seizure of British property and persons on board American vessels, thereby committing a clear violation of the treaty of 1778. But their excuse was that this had been abrogated by the ratification of Jay's treaty, and that the commerce of the United States became thereby the legitimate prey of French cruisers. The course of our resident minister to France, Mr. Monroe, was marked by such passive conduct under these provocations as to render him obnoxious to his own government, and he was accordingly recalled. This gave offense to the French party in the United States, and was also highly resented in France. Subsequently, when General C. C. Pinckney, of South Carolina, a gentleman of known ability and moderation, but of Federalist proclivities, was sent over as Monroe's successor, the French government refused to receive him. He was denied the usual card of hospitality, and was even threatened with the surveillance of the Minister of Police. He repelled these insults with dignity, and with becoming firmness insisted on the protection of the law of nations due to him as the representative of a foreign power. But instead of giving any proper satisfaction for these insults the French government followed them up in January, 1797, by a written notice to Mr. Pinckney to quit the French territory. He retired to Amsterdam, and there awaited further instructions from his own government.

When news of these outrages reached the United States, it occasioned great popular indignation. President Adams convened Congress in extra session on the 15th of May following. In the President's speech to Congress he enlarged with patriotic indignation on the enormity of these proceedings on the part of the French government, and urged prompt measures of redress, and that preparation should be made for hostilities apparently so imminent between the two countries. Yet with admirable prudence, he kept open a door for the renewal of diplomatic relations. In response to his message, Congress took some measures to put the country in a state of defense. The Navy Department was created at this period, and additions were made to our war marine. The President was empowered to raise a provisional army, and the armed vessels of the United States were authorized to capture and bring into port all French vessels committing outrages on American ships or citizens. Washington was again appointed commander-in-chief, with the rank of lieutenant general, and other military preparations were pushed forward with great energy. In the mean time the American Congress acted with commendable dignity and wisdom, authorizing the President, in the interests of peace, to institute a special mission to France, to demand redress and reparation for the injuries complained of. It was in pursuance of this policy that Marshall and his colleagues were nominated.

These circumstances invested this new mission with a peculiarly important and interesting character, and its result was awaited with deep interest throughout the country. The issues of peace or war seemed suspended upon it, and although ultimately no disastrous consequences were actually realized by reason of its failure, its progress and development form one of the most curious and extraordinary chapters in the history of diplomacy.

The American envoys arrived in Paris, October 4, 1797. On the following day they informed the minister of foreign affairs of their arrival, and inquired when he would receive one of their secretaries with the official notification of their credentials. Talleyrand appointed the next day, when their letters of credence were presented and duly acknowledged. A few days later he informed them, through one of his secretaries, that the Directory had called upon him for a report as to the posture of affairs with regard to the United States, that he was then engaged in preparing it, and that it would soon be finished, when he would further inform them. In reply to in-

quiries, he said that the usual cards of hospitality would be sent to them, which were
accordingly received the next day, addressed
suitably to them in their official character.
Thus far, everything denoted a friendly official
reception, and the prompt opening of negotiations. But in less than ten days afterwards
General Pinckney was informed by the clerk
of the American consulate at Paris that he had
learned, through one of Talleyrand's confidential secretaries, that the Directory were highly
incensed at the language and tone of the President's speech to Congress, and that they would
expect and require satisfactory explanations before the envoys could have a public audience;
but that, meantime, certain persons might be
appointed who would confer with them, and
would report to Talleyrand, who had sole
charge of the negotiations.

A few days later, General Pinckney was
waited upon by M. Hottinguer, who was represented to him as a gentleman of credit and
reputation, and who came with a message from
M. Talleyrand. He began by saying that the
French minister had a great regard for the
United States, and was very desirous that there
should be a friendly adjustment of all matters
of difference between the two countries. He
said that he was ready, if it was deemed

proper, to suggest a plan, which Talleyrand expected would answer that purpose. On General Pinckney's encouraging him to proceed, and saying that he was ready to hear, M. Hottinguer continued that the Directory, particularly two of them, were very much exasperated at some parts of President Adams's speech, and that they desired that these should be softened; that this would be necessary before the envoys could be received; that besides this, a sum of money would be required for the use of the Directory, which would be at the disposal of M. Talleyrand, and that a loan to France from the United States would also be expected and insisted upon. M. Hottinguer added that, when these terms were complied with, he had no doubt that the envoys would promptly be received and all differences satisfactorily arranged. The particular passages of the President's speech which were so obnoxious to the Directory, he could not specify, neither the amount of the loan needed, but the tribute for the Directory had been fixed at twelve hundred thousand livres, about fifty thousand pounds sterling, equivalent to two hundred and fifty thousand dollars in coin. To this General Pinckney replied that he would inform his colleagues of what had been proposed, and confer with them as to their answer, and the interview terminated. In their conference the three envoys agreed that General Pinckney should request Hottinguer to make his propositions in writing, in order to avoid misapprehension. Accordingly at the next interview that gentleman brought with him and left with the envoys certain written propositions. He had, however, previously informed Mr. Pinckney that his communication was not directly from M. Talleyrand, but through another agent in whom Talleyrand had great confidence.

On October 20, M. Hottinguer further informed them that M. Bellamy of Hamburg, in the confidence of M. Talleyrand, would call upon them and make all needful explanations. Bellamy came accordingly, and after dwelling on the favorable sentiments entertained by M. Talleyrand toward the United States, announced that minister's desire to aid the envoys in their negotiations by his friendly mediation with the Directory; but said that, in consequence of the displeasure of that body with the President's speech, the Directory had not received or acknowledged them in their representative character, and would not, as yet, authorize M. Talleyrand to hold any communications with them; that on this account M. Talleyrand himself could not see them, but authorized M. Bellamy to make certain propositions to them and report their reply. He added that he held no diplomatic character, and was simply a friend of Talleyrand, enjoying his confidence and wishing to serve him. He designated certain parts of the President's speech as exceptionable, and submitted written propositions as to the proposed treaty. Among these were certain preliminary disavowals and explanations which would be expected, and an article providing that France should be placed in every respect upon the same footing which England occupied under Jay's treaty; there was also a secret clause to the effect that the United States should make a loan to France.

Recurring again to the necessity of removing the dissatisfaction arising from the President's speech, as a preliminary to any negotiation, M. Bellamy said: "Gentlemen, I will not disguise from you that, this satisfaction being made, the essential part of the treaty remains to be adjusted. *Il faut de l'argent. Il faut beaucoup d'argent.*" (It is necessary to pay money, — to pay a great deal of money.)

In a succeeding interview, on the next day, M. Bellamy informed the envoys that he had just been with M. Talleyrand. He said that they were both sensible of the pain the envoys must feel in making the required disavowal as to the President's speech, but that this was an indispensable prerequisite to an official recognition, *unless* means could be found of changing the mind of the Directory; that he had no authority to suggest these means, but that, as a private citizen, he could express the opinion that with money this change of feeling might be effected. He specified the sum which he believed would be accepted, and suggested a convenient mode of raising it. He said that there were thirty - two millions of Dutch rescriptions, worth ten shillings in the pound, which might be assigned to the United States at twenty shillings in the pound. That by the hypothecation of these securities of the Dutch government, the money could be raised to meet the urgent needs of the French government, and that the securities would certainly be paid in full by the former, at their par value, after the war, so that the United States would ultimately lose nothing by the financial operation proposed. He was asked if the *douceur* or tribute to the Directory was to be added to this sum, and he answered in the affirmative. In reply, the ambassadors informed him that while their powers were full and ample to negotiate a treaty with France, they were not authorized to make a loan ; that if that was deemed a *sine qua non* to concluding negotiations, one of their number could return to the United States for

fresh instructions ; and that, if their government should accede to the proposed loan, they
could proceed on that basis ; that meantime the
two other envoys, remaining in France, could
negotiate concerning other questions ; but that
in this interval there must be an entire suspen-
sion of all hostile orders affecting the commerce,
the persons, or the property of the United
States, and of all pending proceedings in respect to captures or seizures already made.

With these propositions M. Bellamy was evidently dissatisfied, saying that they demanded
concessions from France at the very moment
when she, the offended party, was claiming redress for grievances and injuries received, and
that they treated the proposition for a loan as
if it came from the Directory, when in fact it
did not have even the authority of M. Talleyrand, and was only a suggestion from himself,
a private citizen, which they might adopt and
use as a substitute for the painful embarrass-
ment demanded of them in a disavowal of the
President's obnoxious speech.

The envoys replied that they understood the
matter perfectly ; that while the propositions
of a loan, etc., were in form to come from
them, they had proceeded in fact from the
Directory or from their minister, the secretary
of foreign relations. M. Bellamy affected great

concern that the envoys had put from them the only practicable mode of opening the door to full negotiations, saying that the Directory would certainly insist on their terms. The envoys replied that the Directory must take the course which they thought compatible with their duty, while they, on their part, would carefully guard the interests and the honor of their own country. They added that the idea of their apologizing for or disavowing the President's speech could not be considered in a serious light; that such a proceeding would render them ridiculous in the eyes of their own government and of all mankind.

The envoys, in permitting this informal intercourse to go so far, had doubtless been influenced by a strong desire to preserve amicable relations with our ancient ally, and to learn with certainty how far the Directory and Talleyrand were personally and officially implicated in the disgraceful proceeding. Pending these irregular conferences, namely, on the 27th of October, news was received at Paris of the signing of definitive terms of peace between Austria and France. This seemed to give fresh impulse to the desire of the French emissaries to hasten results with the American envoys. Accordingly another visit was made to them by M. Hottinguer. He now complained that they had not been heard from, and said that the government expected to receive propositions from them ; that the Directory was becoming very impatient, and would take very decided steps if the offensive features of the President's speech were not explained or softened. He alluded to the peace just concluded, and said that it ought " to produce a change in the attitude of the envoys; that France had determined to take higher grounds with the United States and all other neutral nations, which must aid France or be treated as enemies." The American envoys replied that they had considered the whole aspect of the case very fully, and that the recent peace would effect no change in their attitude. M. Hottinguer, after enlarging on the now augmented power and resources of France, returned again to the subject of money. He said: " Gentlemen, you do not speak to the point. It is money. It is expected that you will offer money." They replied that they had already answered explicitly on that point. " No," said he, " you have not. What is your answer? " They replied: " *It is No. No ; not a sixpence.*" The conversation continued some time, during which the private advance of money and the public loan were pressed in a variety of forms. M. Hottinguer, in conclusion, said that he would communicate as nearly as he could the sub-

8

stance of what had passed, either to M. Bellamy or to the minister.

Up to this time the envoys had had no personal interview with M. Talleyrand. They had only seen him once, and that for a short time. They did not doubt, however, that these mediaries from him, with whom they had conferred, were his agents, sent by him to effect by indirection and false representations objects in gaining which he did not like to appear directly. These suspicions were soon fully verified. M. Talleyrand furnished conclusive evidence that these terms, so persistently urged by his unofficial agents, did really proceed from himself.

Later in October another messenger, still unofficial, from M. Talleyrand, appeared on the stage, a M. Hautval, said to be a French gentleman of respectable character, for they were "all honorable men." Hautval called on Mr. Gerry, and informed him that M. Talleyrand had expected to see the American envoys frequently in private intercourse, and to confer with them individually as to their mission, and that he had been authorized to make this known to them. On Mr. Gerry informing his colleagues of this message, Messrs. Pinckney and Marshall said that, as they were not acquainted with M. Talleyrand, they could not see the propriety of their calling on him; but Mr. Gerry, having formed an acquaintance with him in the United States, might properly be expected, according to the custom in France, to call upon him. A few days afterward Mr. Gerry, in company with M. Hautval, did call upon M. Talleyrand. M. Talleyrand began the conversation. He said that the Directory had passed an *arrêt*, in which they renewed their demand for an explanation of the President's speech, etc., *but, on their offering money*, he thought that he could prevent the effect of the *arrêt*. Mr. Gerry informed the minister that they were not authorized to offer money. In that case, M. Talleyrand replied, they could take the power to do so, and he proposed that they should take this step. Mr. Gerry, continuing to allege the want of power, repeated what had been said in previous conferences, that one of his colleagues might return to America for instructions on that head provided the other objects of their negotiations could, in the mean time, be considered. Mr. Gerry then expressed a wish that M. Talleyrand would confer with his colleagues. M. Talleyrand replied that he should be happy to confer with the envoys individually, but " *that this matter about the money must be settled directly without sending to America;* " that he would not communicate the *arrêt* for a week ; and that if they could adjust the diffi, culty as to the speech, an application would be sent to the United States for the loan.   Two conclusions are manifest from this statement by M. Talleyrand. First, that he was perfectly aware that his agents had proposed and insisted on *the payment of money, as a bribe,* into his own hands, as a condition precedent to opening formal negotiations, — the same conclusion is also to be drawn from his opening statement, to wit, that their offering money would have the effect of suspending the *arrêt.* Second, that the smaller sum named, to wit, the *douceur* of two hundred and fifty thousand dollars, must be advanced in cash, "directly" and "before sending to America," a transaction which doubtless he knew well that the financial credit of the envoys could accomplish.

In another visit, after Mr. Gerry's interview with Talleyrand, Messrs. Hottinguer and Bellamy announced to the envoys that, "if the terms already offered to them should be rejected, and war should ensue, the fate of Venice might befall the United States." " Perhaps," said M. Bellamy, "you believe that, in returning and exposing to your countrymen the unreasonableness of the demands of this government, you will unite them in their resistance to those demands. You are mistaken. You ought to know that the diplomatic skill of France and the means she possesses in your country are sufficient to enable her, with the aid of the French party in America, to throw the blame which will attend the rupture of the negotiations on the 'Federalists,' as you term yourselves, but on the 'British party,' as France terms you ; and you may assure yourselves that this will be done." [1]

Such haughty insolence produced its natural effect. It induced the envoys to do at length what they would have been well justified in doing sooner, — declining to hold further indirect intercourse with a government which had shown itself so destitute of truth, and so incapable of acting with openness and honor. They accordingly announced this determination to M. Talleyrand. Yet in spite of it other attempts were frequently made to draw them into the like irregular and unofficial intercourse, but fortunately altogether without effect.

One of the methods resorted to for compassing this object was singular enough. One Beaumarchais, a very wealthy French citizen residing in Paris, was a client of Mr. Marshall, whose professional services he had secured in the prosecution of a claim which Beaumarchais asserted against the State of Virginia for re-

[1] Waite's *American State Papers*, vol. iii. p. 214.

covery of the large sum of a hundred and forty-
five thousand pounds sterling, alleged to be due
for military supplies furnished to that State
during the Revolutionary War. Beaumarchais
had obtained a judgment for the amount in the
lower court, but from this judgment an appeal
had been taken to a higher court, and the final
result was yet undetermined. He had called
on Mr. Marshall, and had entertained him and
his colleagues at dinner. Beaumarchais was a
large capitalist and an intriguer of great cleverness. M. Bellamy saw in these circumstances
a gleam of hope for raising the much-coveted
douceur, which, as M. Talleyrand's agent, he
was bent upon securing. He had little difficulty in bringing M. Beaumarchais into his
views, and on the 17th of December M. Bellamy informed Marshall that Beaumarchais had
consented, provided his claim should be admitted, to sacrifice fifty thousand pounds sterling
of it as the *douceur* so often demanded; so that
the payment of that sum could not work any
loss to the American government. This proposition was not entertained, the envoys regarding it as an attempt to renew the unofficial
negotiations. Mr. Marshall makes the following allusion to it in his journal : —

"Having been originally the counsel of M. de
Beaumarchais I had determined, and so I had in-

formed General Pinckney, that I would not, by my voice, establish any agreement in his favor, but that I would positively oppose any admission of the claim of any French citizen if not accompanied with an admission of the claims of American citizens for property captured and condemned for want of a *rôle d'équipage.*" [1]

Mr. Gerry's intercourse with these messengers of Talleyrand seems to have been more frequent and intimate than that of his colleagues. There was one on the 17th of December, in the presence of M. Bellamy, in which Mr. Gerry said to M. Talleyrand that M. Bellamy had informed him of some propositions coming from him, Talleyrand, referring to the gratuity of £50,000 and the purchase of the Dutch rescriptions, to which he could give no reply, etc. M. Talleyrand said that what M. Bellamy had told him was true; that Bellamy could always be depended upon; that he would put his proposals in writing. This he accordingly did, but after he had shown them to Mr. Gerry he destroyed the paper. These proposals referred to the purchase of the Dutch securities, but did not allude to the gratuity. That was doubtless to be the special work of his agents.

---

[1] This debt to Beaumarchais was incurred by the State of Virginia during the war of the Revolution, in the purchase of supplies for the continental army, and was afterward assumed and paid in full by the United States government.

The envoys now resolved that they would address M. Talleyrand by letter, and lay before him in that explicit form the special objects of their mission, discussing the points at issue between the two governments just as if they had been officially received; also, that on the refusal or failure of the French government to open negotiations with them, they would demand their passports and return to the United States. This letter, prepared by Marshall, was a full and clear statement of the whole subject, and has ever been regarded as a model state paper.[1] Before sending it, however, the three thought it wise to request a personal interview with Talleyrand. He readily assented and appointed a day to receive them. On this occasion he said in substance to the envoys, that the Directory would require some proof, on the part of the United States government, of a friendly disposition towards France, preparatory to opening negotiations, and alluded very plainly to a loan as furnishing that proof. They replied by repeating that they had no power to make a loan, and that such an act would be inconsistent with the neutrality of the United States, and might involve them in a war with Great Britain. Talleyrand urged that foreign ministers must often, in their dis-

[1] Waite's *State Papers*, vol. iii. p. 219.

cretion, assume responsibility for the sake of
the public good ; that the loan could be so dis-
guised as to prevent any violation of their
neutral obligations to England ; and that if
they really desired to conciliate France and accomplish the object of their mission, they would
have no difficulty in finding the means to do so.
He added, by way of complaint, that the envoys had not visited him as he expected, and
that, although the Directory had not given them
an official audience, there was no reason why
they might not have seen him often and found
opportunity in personal interviews to remove
all difficulties in the way of their mutual intercourse. Mr. Marshall replied with dignity that
it was not a matter of the least concern to
them whether they had an interview with the
Directory or not; that they were perfectly in-
different in that matter; that they had expected
and demanded that their official character
should be acknowledged, and that they would
not undertake to act in that character until
they should have been so recognized. Mr.
Marshall further said that to lend or to raise
money for France to enable her to carry on the
war then waging with England would be giving aid to her and taking part in the war, and
that their doing so without special authority
was out of the question.

After an interval of a fortnight M. Talley-rand transmitted his answer to the above-mentioned letter of the envoys, in which, after a needless repetition of what he had previously said, he proceeded : " The Executive Directory is disposed to treat with that one of the three whose opinions are presumed to be more impartial, and to promise in the course of the explanations more of that reciprocal confidence which is indispensable." This was intended to designate Mr. Gerry, who was supposed to be more favorable to the loan to France than his colleagues. To this it was replied by Mr. Marshall that the powers of the envoys were joint ; that no one of them could conclude negotiations in which it was intended that all should participate ; nor could the other two decline duties which were thus plainly conferred upon them all by their government. They concluded by demanding passports for the whole or any number of them, which should be accompanied with letters of safe conduct.

It was no doubt intended and desired by M. Talleyrand that Messrs. Marshall and Pinckney should voluntarily retire, on receipt of this letter making the invidious distinction between them and Mr. Gerry. For, in a letter to Mr. Gerry, dated April 3, he wrote: "I suppose, sir, that Messrs. Pinckney and Marshall have thought it useful and proper, in consequence of the intimations which the end of my note of the 18th of March last presents, to quit the territory of the Republic." As the envoys, however, had previously demanded their passports, this inhospitality was merely a gratuitous indignity, showing evidently a wish for their departure, but an unwillingness to take the responsibility of helping them away. They, upon their part, seeing that a proper self-respect and due regard for the honor and dignity of their country forbade them to remain longer, were indeed anxious to return to the United States; but they were resolved not to sneak away, as Talleyrand ventured to suppose that they had done, but to demand the official *exequatur* and the protection of the usual safeguards against capture, to which, by the custom of nations, they were entitled. Marshall told Talleyrand that the conduct of the French government was in violation of the laws and customs of civilized nations observed toward foreign nations. He replied that Marshall was not a foreign minister but only an Amercan citizen, who must obtain his passports, like all others, through the American consul. Mr. Marshall repelled this false and offensive assertion, remarking sarcastically that Talleyrand's ignorance of the laws of nations could alone excuse a statement so destitute of foundation; he said that he derived his character as foreign minister not from M. Talleyrand or the French government, but from the United States, which had conferred it upon him; that though the Directory might refuse to treat with him and his colleagues, still they held their public position independently of France, and were entitled to leave like other ministers with their passports and letters of safe conduct. To this Talleyrand made the impertinent reply that if Marshall wanted a passport he must send in his name, stature, age, and complexion to the American consul, who would obtain one for him; and that, as to a safe conduct, it was unnecessary, as he would incur no risk from French cruisers.[1]

Though thus treated with studied rudeness, Pinckney and Marshall persisted in their demand, and the passports were at last sent to them. Marshall left Paris on the 12th of April, but Mr. Pinckney, with some difficulty, obtained permission from the French government, in consequence of the ill-health of his daughter, who had accompanied him to France, to remain longer. As to Mr. Gerry, who, as Talleyrand said, had "manifested himself more disposed to lend a favorable ear to everything which might reconcile the two republics," he was in-

[1] Marshall's *Journal. American State Papers*, vol. iii. p. 394

duced by threats of immediate war by France against the United States to remain in Paris. It was said that, although warmly urged to enter into negotiations with the Directory after his colleagues left, he refused to do so. His conduct, however, provoked severe criticism at home and lowered his character with his countrymen, though he was generally accredited with fair intentions.

The dispatches of the envoys to their government reported fully what had occurred in their attempt to execute their mission. These were now communicated in a message to Congress from the President, were published in full in the newspapers of the day, and were thence transferred into the English papers. They reached France, in due time, and created a profound sensation. Talleyrand took early measures to forestall their effect, and hastened to disavow the shameful part which the simple recital of the facts assigned to him in the transaction. In the publication of the official papers the American secretary of state had used the initials X. Y. Z. for the names of Messrs. Hottinguer, Bellamy, and Hautval, as they had requested the envoys not to make public their real names. This circumstance enabled the wily French secretary to resort to the trick of affecting entire ignorance of the persons thus referred to, whom he designated as "intriguers," who had deceived the envoys. He even had the audacity to inquire by letter of Mr. Gerry, still in Paris, as to these persons, and requested to be furnished with their names!

"I cannot observe without surprise," he said, "that intriguers have profited by the insulated condition in which the envoys of the United States have kept themselves, to make proposals and hold conversations, the object of which was evidently to deceive you." This to Mr. Gerry, to whom Talleyrand had given the distinct assurance that "what M. Bellamy had said to him, as coming from him (Talleyrand), was true, and that he might always be relied upon;" to Mr. Gerry, who had heard the proposals which had been made by these agents substantially renewed by the minister himself, and who was present when General Pinckney told Talleyrand that his suggestions were considered by the envoys as substantially the same as those made by Messrs. Hottinguer and Bellamy, the men whom he now styled officious intriguers, but whose statements he had not denied or disavowed at that time! M. Talleyrand further published in the "Redacteur," the official gazette, a labored defense and reply to these dispatches, characterized by true Machiavellian dissimulation and unscrupulous mendacity, which it is not necessary here to repeat.

Mr. Marshall arrived in New York on the 17th of June, after a long voyage. This interval had afforded time for the American public to read the published dispatches of our envoys and acquaint themselves with the history of a mission so extraordinary and so disgraceful to France. He found an intense indignation prevailing throughout the country, and he was received with warm enthusiasm wherever he appeared. All parties and classes united in cordial approbation of the dignity, ability, and manly spirit he had displayed throughout the mission.

The history of these events, so soon as known, had naturally augmented the strength of the Federalists and weakened the Republicans. Mr. Jefferson viewed this state of things with great jealousy. He was perhaps the only prominent public character in the country who remarked with discontent the honors accorded to Marshall as one who had conducted himself, in such a trying ordeal, with admirable wisdom and firmness, and who certainly deserved the grateful plaudits of his countrymen. In a letter written at this crisis to Mr. Madison, Mr. Jefferson, after mentioning the arrival of Marshall at New York, says : —

"I have postponed my own departure from Philadelphia in order to see if that circumstance would produce any new projects. No doubt he [Marshall] there received more than hints from Hamilton as to the tone required to be assumed; yet I apprehend he is not hot enough for his friends. Livingston came with him from New York. Marshall told him they had no idea in France of a war with us; that Talleyrand sent passports to him and Pinckney, but none to Gerry; upon this Gerry stayed, without explaining to them the reason. He wrote, however, to the President by Marshall, who knew nothing of the contents of the letter, so that there must have been a previous understanding between Talleyrand and Gerry.[1] Marshall was received here [Philadelphia] with the utmost *éclat*. The secretary of state and many carriages, with all the city cavalry, went to Frankford to meet him, and on his arrival here, in the evening, the bells rung till late in the night, and immense crowds were collected to see and make part of the show, which was circuitously paraded through the streets before he was set down at the city tavern." "All this," Jefferson proceeds, "was to secure him to their views, that he might say nothing which would oppose the game they had been playing. Since his

---

[1] Mr. Flanders says, in his *Lives of the Chief Justices*, vol. ii. p. 382: "Marshall could not have told Livingston this, because Gerry had agreed with Talleyrand to remain, had told his colleagues that he intended to remain, and this, too, before the passports were sent. His not receiving a passport had nothing to do with his staying. It would have been sent, had he demanded it."

arrival I can hear nothing directly from him, while they are disseminating through the town things as from him diametrically opposite to what he said to Livingston." [1]

A public dinner was given to Marshall by members of both houses of Congress, then in session, " as an evidence of affection for his person, and of their grateful approbation of the patriotic firmness with which he sustained the dignity of his country during his important mission."

It was at this dinner, and by way of indignant rebuke of the infamous invitation by Talleyrand to our envoys to resort to a bribe in order to obtain a hearing by the French government, that the sentiment, so happily expressed, was offered and cordially welcomed: "*Millions for defense, but not a cent for tribute,*" a sentiment so entirely in unison with the pulsations of every patriotic heart that it was eagerly caught up and quickly wafted through the length and breadth of the land with every demonstration of popular enthusiasm.

On his return to Virginia Marshall was not less warmly welcomed by all parties. He immediately resumed his law practice, which was always his most congenial employment, and from which he hoped now to be no more with-

[1] Jefferson's *Works*, vol. iv. p. 249.

drawn. But it was obvious that the time for that coveted retirement from public life was not yet come. Little as he desired it, he was to be remanded to the political arena by influences to which he was constrained to yield.

CHAPTER VIII.

How fully Marshall enjoyed the confidence of Washington, is proved by the facts that Washington offered him a seat in the cabinet as attorney general, and also an important foreign mission. Both these positions he had been obliged to decline. But the singularly responsible, difficult, and delicate task, which he had accepted upon the nomination of Mr. Adams, had been so well performed that further recognition of his ability was inevitable. In the summer of 1798, a vacancy occurred on the bench of the Supreme Court of the United States, and Adams resolved to appoint Mr. Marshall to fill it. He wrote to his secretary of state, Mr. Pickering, who was disposed to prefer Bushrod Washington, an eminent lawyer and a favorite nephew of the ex-President: "General Marshall or Bushrod Washington will succeed Judge Wilson, if you have not some other gentleman to propose who, in your opinion, can better promote the public honor and interest. Marshall is first in age, rank, and public services; probably not second in talents." In a subsequent letter to the secretary, he further said : —

" The name, the connections, the character, the merit, and abilities of Mr. Washington are greatly respected, but I still think General Marshall ought to be preferred. Of the three envoys [to France] the conduct of Marshall alone has been entirely satisfactory and ought to be marked by the most decided approbation of the public. He has raised the American people in their own esteem ; and if the influence of truth and justice, reason and argument, is not lost in Europe, he has raised the consideration of the United States in that quarter. He is older at the bar than Mr. Washington, and you and I know by experience that seniority at the bar is nearly as much regarded as it is in the army. If Mr. Marshall should decline, I should next think of Mr. Washington." [1]

Insurmountable considerations, as Mr. Marshall wrote to the secretary of state, obliged him to decline this honor, and the appointment accordingly fell to Bushrod Washington, very fortunately, as it turned out, for Washington made an excellent judge and Marshall soon became chief justice.

One of the chief reasons, doubtless the con-

[1] Adams's *Works*, vol. viii. p. 597.

trolling one, which at this period (Sept. 26, 1798) induced Marshall to decline the office thus tendered him was, that he had been induced, much against his will, to become a candidate for Congress. He had been invited to Mount Vernon, and there had been subjected to such earnest personal solicitation by General Washington that he had at last consented to accept a candidacy which he would have gladly shunned.

" I learned with much pleasure," wrote Washington to his nephew, Bushrod Washington, "from the postscript of your letter, of General Marshall's intention to make me a visit. I wish it of all things, and it is from the ardent desire I have to see him that I have not delayed a moment to express it, lest, if he should have intended it on his way to Frederic, and [should] hear of my indisposition, he might change his route. I can add with sincerity and truth, that if you can make it comport with your business I should be exceedingly happy to see you along with him. The crisis is important. The temper of the people in this State, at least in some places, is so violent and outrageous, that I wish to converse with General Marshall and yourself on the elections, which must come soon." [1]

This visit to Mount Vernon, apart from all public considerations, seems to have afforded

[1] *Washington's Writings*, vol. xi. p. 292.

Washington great pleasure. Mr. Paulding has given us a pleasant memorial of it, with some amusing personal incidents. Washington sometimes related the anecdote to this effect: —

"They came on horseback, and for convenience or some other purpose had bestowed their wardrobes in the same pair of saddle-bags, each party occupying his side. On their arrival at Mount Vernon, wet to the skin by a shower of rain, they were shown into a chamber to change their garments. One unlocked his side of the bag, and the first thing he drew forth was a black bottle of whiskey. He insisted that this was his companion's repository, but on unlocking the other there was found a huge twist of tobacco, a few pieces of corn bread, and the complete equipment of a wagoner's pack-saddle! They had exchanged saddle-bags with some travelers on the way, and finally made their appearance in borrowed clothes, that fitted them most ludicrously. The general was highly diverted, and amused himself with anticipating the dismay of the wagoner, when he discovered this oversight of the men of law." [1]

Notwithstanding the great popularity of Mr. Marshall and the *éclat* of his conduct in the recent French mission, his election to Congress was warmly opposed by the Democratic party, with Mr. Jefferson at its head, and the contest was a severe one. Party feeling was highly

[1] Paulding's *Life of Washington*, vol. ii. p. 191.

inflamed, especially in Virginia. Marshall was severely arraigned as the advocate of a strong monarchical government, as a consolidationist, etc. One of the means used to defeat him was a report, industriously circulated in the district, that Patrick Henry, who belonged to the opposite political party, and whose name was a pillar of strength throughout the State, was opposed to his election. It is highly honorable to Colonel Henry that, when informed of the use thus made of his name, he promptly addressed a letter to his friend Mr. Blair, of Richmond, in which he refuted the statement and thus spoke of General Marshall : —

" General Marshall and his colleagues exhibited the American character as respectable. France in the period of her most triumphant fortune beheld them as unappalled. Her threats left them, as she found them, mild, temperate, firm. Can it be thought that, with these sentiments, I should utter anything tending to prejudice General Marshall's election ? Very far from it indeed. Independently of the high gratification I felt from his public ministry, he ever stood high in my esteem as a private citizen. His temper and disposition were always pleasant. His talents and integrity unquestioned. These things are sufficient to place that gentleman far above any competition in the district for Congress; but when you add the particular information and insight which he has gained, and is able to communicate to our public councils, it is really astonishing that even blindness itself should hesitate in the choice. But it is to be observed that the efforts of France are to loosen the confidence of the people everywhere in the public functionaries, and to blacken characters most eminently distinguished for virtue, talents, and public confidence; thus smoothing the way to conquest, or those claims of superiority as abhorrent to my mind as conquest, from whatever quarter they may come.

"Tell Marshall I love him, because he felt and acted as a republican, as an American. The story of the Scotch merchants and old tories voting for him is too stale, childish, and foolish, and is a French *finesse;* an appeal to prejudice, not to reason and good sense. As to the particular words stated by you and said to come from me, I do not recollect saying them, but certain I am, I never said anything derogatory to General Marshall; but, on the contrary, I really should give him my vote for Congress, preferably to any citizen in the State at this juncture, one only excepted, and that one is in another line." [1]

From a political opponent, of very strong Democratic predilections, this was certainly a very handsome and a very unusual tribute.

Another unfounded and ungenerous report was diligently propagated in the canvass, and was keenly felt by Mr. Marshall. He alludes

[1] This is supposed to be a reference to Washington, then just appointed general-in-chief of the army to be raised for resisting the aggressions of France.

to it in a letter to General Washington, which, with the brief reply of the latter, we here insert: —

" You may possibly have seen," says Marshall, " a paragraph in a late publication stating that several important offices in the gift of the executive, and among others that of secretary of state, had been obtainable by me. Few of the unpleasant occurrences produced by my declaration as a candidate for Congress, and they have been very abundant, have given me more real chagrin than this. To make a parade of proffered offices is a vanity which I trust I do not possess, but to boast of one never in my power would argue a littleness of mind at which I ought to blush. I know not how the author may have acquired his information, but I beg leave to assure you that he never received it directly nor indirectly from me. I had no previous knowledge that such a publication was designed, or I should certainly have suppressed so much of it as relates to this subject. The writer was unquestionably actuated by a wish to serve me, and by resentment at the various malignant calumnies which have been so profusely bestowed on me. One of these was, that I only wished a seat in Congress for the purpose of obtaining some office, which my devotion to the administration might procure. To repel this was obviously the motive of the indiscreet publication I so much regret. A wish to rescue myself in your opinion from the imputation of an idle vanity, which forms, if I know myself, no part of my character, will, I trust, apologize for the trouble this explanation may give you." [1]

It appears from the brief and gratifying letter of Washington in reply that Marshall's explanation was needless.

"I am sorry to find," Washington wrote, " that the publication you allude to should have given you a moment's disquietude. I can assure you it made no impression on my mind of the tendency apprehended by you."

But in spite of the best efforts which Marshall's opponents could put forth, the Richmond district elected him. Though the majority was small, the result afforded high gratification to his friends. Washington wrote to his nephew, Bushrod Washington : " The election of General Lee and Marshall is grateful to my feelings. I wish, however, both of them had been elected by greater majorities; but they are elected, and that alone is pleasing. As the tide is turned I hope it will come in with a full flow, but this will not happen if there is any relaxation on the part of the Federalists."

Congress convened in December, 1799, and Marshall took his seat in the House of Representatives, " a body," says Mr. Horace Binney, " perhaps never exceeded in the number of its

---

[1] *Washington's Writings,* vol. xi. p 424.

accomplished debaters, or in the spirit with which they contended for the prize of public approbation."[1] It was the last which convened in Philadelphia.

In view of Washington's extreme solicitude to see Marshall in Congress, and of the great pleasure his election afforded to his illustrious chief and friend, it is affecting to reflect that one of the first duties he was called to perform was to announce in the House the death of that great man, — "the hero, the patriot, and the sage of America;" an unexpected calamity, which plunged a whole country into the profoundest grief. A rumor of Washington's death had reached Philadelphia not long after the event occurred, but it was most earnestly hoped that it was unfounded. Later intelligence, however, dissipated this slender hope. On the next day, the 19th of December, "with suppressed voice and deep emotion," Mr. Marshall addressed the chair, as follows: —

"The melancholy event, which was yesterday announced with doubt, has been rendered but too certain. Our Washington is no more! the hero, the patriot, the sage of America, the man on whom in times of danger every eye was turned and all hopes were placed, lives now only in his own great actions, and in the hearts of an affectionate and afflicted people.

[1] Binney's *Eulogy on Marshall*, p. 52.

"If, sir, it had even not been usual openly to testify respect for the memory of those whom Heaven
has selected as its instruments for dispensing good to
man, yet, such has been the uncommon worth and
such the extraordinary incidents which have marked
the life of him whose loss we all deplore, that the
whole American nation, impelled by the same feelings, would call, with one voice, for a public manifestation of that sorrow which is so deep and so universal.

"More than any other individual, and as much as
to one individual was possible, has he contributed to
found this, our wide-spreading empire, and to give to
the western world independence and freedom.

"Having effected the great object for which he
was placed at the head of our armies, we have seen
him convert the sword into the ploughshare, and
sink the soldier in the citizen.

"When the debility of our federal system had become manifest, and the bonds which connected this
vast continent were dissolving, we have seen him
the chief of those patriots who formed for us a constitution which, by preserving the Union, will, I trust,
substantiate and perpetuate those blessings which
our Revolution had promised to bestow.

"In obedience to the general voice of his country,
calling him to preside over a great people, we have
seen him once more quit the retirement he loved, and
in a season more stormy and tempestuous than war
itself, with calm and wise determination, pursue the
great interests of the nation, and contribute, more

than any other could contribute, to the establishment of that system of policy which will, I trust, yet preserve our peace, our honor, and our independence.

" Having been twice unanimously chosen the chief magistrate of a free people, we have seen him, at a time when his reëlection with universal suffrage could not be doubted, afford to the world a rare instance of moderation, by withdrawing from his high station to the peaceful walks of private life.

" However the public confidence may change and the public affection fluctuate with respect to others, with respect to him, they have, in war and in peace, in public and in private life, been as steady as his own firm mind, and as constant as his own exalted virtues.

" Let us, then, Mr. Speaker, pay the last tribute of respect and affection to our departed friend. Let the grand council of the nation display those sentiments which the nation feels. For this purpose I hold in my hand some resolutions which I take the liberty of offering to the House."

These resolutions,[1] after a preamble stating the death of General Washington, were in the following terms :—

" *Resolved*, that this House will wait on the President in condolence of this mournful event.

[1] They were prepared by General Henry Lee, who, happening not to be in his place when the melancholy intelligence was received and first mentioned in the House, placed them in the hands of the member who moved them.

" *Resolved,* that the Speaker's chair be shrouded with black, and the members and officers of the House wear black, during the session.

" *Resolved,* that a committee, in conjunction with one from the Senate, be appointed to consider the most suitable manner of paying honors to the memory of the man first in war, first in peace, and first in the hearts of his fellow-citizens."

In the deliberations of the House of Representatives Mr. Marshall, who was ever "swift to hear, but slow to speak," was constrained by circumstances to take a somewhat active part. His reputation for ability, his experience in public affairs, both at home and abroad, and the earnest desire of members to learn his views, forced him to occupy the floor oftener than he desired. On all questions involving international and constitutional law he soon became the leading authority; to discuss these was, with him, to exhaust them, for he left nothing more to be said. Of such a character was the question raised by a resolution offered by Mr. Livingston of New York, arraigning the President's conduct in surrendering to the British authorities, under a clause of Jay's treaty, one Thomas Nash, better known under his assumed name of Jonathan Robbins, claimed as a British subject upon a charge of murder committed on the high seas on board an English frigate. Robbins falsely claimed to be an American citizen and to have been impressed into the British navy. He was arrested and imprisoned for his alleged crime in Charleston, South Carolina, at the instance of the British consul. The British minister made a requisition on the President for his surrender as a fugitive from justice. Under the provisions of the treaty, the United States judge in Charleston was advised by President Adams to surrender him to the British authorities, provided the evidence against him was such as, by the laws of this country, would justify his commitment for trial if the crime had been laid within the jurisdiction of the United States. The evidence of his criminality being satisfactory to the federal court, he was accordingly remanded into the custody of the British consul, was tried by a court-martial, found guilty, and executed. He confessed before his death that he was an Irishman.

This was the first case of the extradition of an alleged criminal arising under international law, recognized and enforced by treaty. Great popular excitement prevailed in the country in consequence of the surrender, inasmuch as the man alleged himself to be an American citizen, who had been unlawfully imprisoned and had committed the homicide in an attempt to free himself from an illegal detention. But it was conceded at length, in the course of the debate in Congress, that he was not an American citizen, and that he had been guilty of the crime for which he had suffered death.

Mr. Marshall defended the course of the President in a close, argumentative speech, in which he maintained, —

I. That the case came within the plain language of the treaty.

II. That it was a question of executive and not of judicial cognizance.

III. That the President could not be justly chargeable with any interference with the judicial department of the government.

In the discussion and defense of these propositions he was eminently successful, so much so, indeed, that although the case had become a party question, and had warmly enlisted party feelings, many of the Republicans voted with Marshall, and the resolutions of censure were lost by the decided vote of thirty-five ayes to sixty-one noes. It was by Marshall that public opinion was thus effectually changed, — a result not often achieved by any number of speeches in times of extreme partisan excitement. Mr. Binney says of it: —

" The speech which he delivered upon this question is believed to be the only one that he ever revised, and it was worthy of the case. It has all the merits, and nearly all the weight, of a judicial sentence. It is throughout inspired by the purest reason and the most copious and accurate learning. It separates the executive from the judicial power by a line so distinct and a discrimination so wise, that all can perceive and approve it. It demonstrated that the surrender was an act of political power, which belonged to the executive; and by excluding all such power by the grant of the constitution to the judiciary, it prepared a pillow of repose for that department, where the success of the opposite argument would have planted thorns." [1]

We cannot afford space for this great argument, but we make room for an extract, which embodies such fairness, such a sense of justice, and such clearness of argument, as to deserve preservation.

" The gentleman from Pennsylvania [Mr. Gallatin] has said that an impressed American seaman, who should commit homicide for the purpose of liberating himself from the vessel in which he was confined, ought not to be given up as a murderer. In this I concur entirely with that gentleman. I believe the opinion to be unquestionably correct, as are the reasons he has given in support of it. I never heard any American avow a contrary sentiment, nor do I believe a contrary sentiment can find a place in the bosom of an American. I cannot pretend, and do

[1] *Eulogy on Marshall*, pp. 53. 54.

10

not pretend, to know the opinion of the executive on
this subject, because I have never heard the opinions of that department; but I feel the most perfect
conviction, founded on the general conduct of the
government, that it could never surrender an impressed American to the nation which, in making the
impressment, committed a national injury. This belief is in no degree shaken by the conduct of the
executive in this particular case.

"The President has decided that a murder, committed on board a British frigate on the high seas, is
within the jurisdiction of that nation, and consequently within the twenty - seventh article of its
treaty with the United States. He therefore directed
Thomas Nash to be delivered to the British minister,
if satisfactory evidence of the murder should be adduced; the sufficiency of the evidence was submitted
entirely to the judge. If Thomas Nash had committed a murder, the decision was that he should be
surrendered to the British minister; but if he had not
committed a murder, he was not to be surrendered.
Had Thomas Nash been an impressed American, the
homicide on board the Hermione would most certainly
not have been a murder. The act of impressing an
American is an act of lawless violence. The con-
finement on board the vessel is a continuation of the
violence and an additional outrage. Death committed
within the United States, in resisting such violence,
is not murder, and the person giving the wound cannot be treated as a murderer. Thomas Nash was
only to be delivered up to justice on such evidence

us, had the fact been committed within the United States, would be sufficient to have induced his commitment and trial for murder. Of consequence, the decision of the President was so expressed as to exclude the case of an impressed American liberating himself by homicide."

The full information concerning the facts of the case, disclosed by this speech, and the candor and calmness with which the whole subject was treated, produced a marked effect upon public opinion, and went far to silence the fierce denunciation which a misapprehension of those facts had occasioned.

A striking anecdote is related of the extraordinary effect produced by the speech of Mr. Marshall on this occasion, during its delivery. The able and accomplished Albert Gallatin, then a member of Congress, at first warmly advocated the resolutions of Mr. Livingston, in an opening speech. When Mr. Marshall arose to reply it was at first Gallatin's intention to answer him. He took his position near Marshall, while that gentleman was speaking, and busied himself in making notes of the argument. But it was observed that, as the speaker proceeded in his usual lucid order, Mr. Gallatin did not make very satisfactory progress, and at length, pushing aside his papers and pencil, he retired to the rear of the hall, where he walked up and

down, keeping himself, however, within sight
and hearing of the orator, by whom his attention was riveted. One of Gallatin's friends,
who knew that he was expected to reply, approached him and inquired why he had ceased
to take notes, asking if he did not mean to
speak. Mr. Gallatin answered, " I do not."
" Why not ? " demanded his interlocutor. " Because I *cannot*," was the reply. " If you can, I
wish you would. There is absolutely no reply
to make, for *his speech is unanswerable.*"

Mr. Marshall earned also, at this session of
Congress, the proud distinction of placing the
obligations of duty and right far above party
feelings and the behests of party discipline.
No measure of policy during the Adams administration, of which Marshall was a strong
supporter, was more warmly associated with
party feeling, and more vigorously defended by
the party zeal of the President's friends, than
the Alien and Sedition laws, passed at a previous session of Congress when Mr. Marshall
was not a member. It was now proposed to
repeal the second section of the latter act,
which formed the sedition feature of the law.
Mr. Marshall honestly disapproved of it and
voted for its repeal, while the names of all those
with whom he generally consorted and acted
are recorded on the opposite side. It has long

since been generally conceded that these acts were gross blunders, the offspring of excited partisan feeling. Marshall's cool judicial sense made him fully cognizant of their objectionable character, and he could not be driven by the party whip to support them. He was never afraid to do right, and did not pause to consider whether he would have to stand alone in his course or not. Mindful of the lesson taught in Holy Writ, he would "not follow a multitude to do evil." He always preferred the right to the popular side, and acted like Henry Clay in the matter of the annexation of Texas, when that upright statesman said, while voting against an act approved by a large majority of his countrymen, but which he honestly condemned: "I would rather be right than be President;" a declaration which, by the way, probably cost Clay his election to the presidency.

Congress adjourned on the 14th of May, 1800, and Marshall, having been again invited by President Adams to a seat in the reorganized cabinet, accepted the post of secretary of state, and consequently resigned his place in Congress.

CHAPTER IX.

IN MR. ADAMS'S CABINET.

1800-1801.

ON the reorganization of the cabinet of President Adams, Mr. Marshall was nominated by the President to the war department, which had been lately vacated by the resignation of General James McHenry. Mr. Marshall had not been consulted concerning this nomination, nor indeed had he received any intimation that General McHenry was to retire. He declined the appointment. But almost immediately afterwards, Mr. Pickering having been removed by the President from the state department, Mr. Marshall, on the renewed invitation of President Adams, accepted that position, and Mr. Dexter was appointed secretary of war. Although this re-arrangement was occasioned by very decided differences of opinion and of policy between the President and his secretaries as to certain public questions, especially those affecting our foreign relations, in respect to which Mr. Marshall agreed with Mr. Adams,

it worked no diminution of the regard theretofore entertained by the discarded secretaries
towards their successors. Mr. Wolcott, who,
though sharing in a great degree the sentiments of his retiring colleagues, yet retained
his place, at the President's request, as head
of the treasury department, wrote thus at the
time to Fisher Ames: —

"Let me not be suspected of entertaining a harsh
opinion that the gentlemen lately appointed to office
are not independent men. I highly respect and esteem them both, and consider their acceptance of
their offices as the best evidence of their patriotism.
. . . I consider General Marshall and Mr. Dexter
as more than secretaries, — as state conservators, —
the value of whose services ought to be estimated not
only by the good that they do, but by the mischief
they have prevented. If I am not mistaken, however, General Marshall will find himself out of his
proper element." [1]

But in this prophecy Mr. Wolcott was himself mistaken, for Mr. Adams wrote: "My
new minister, Marshall, did all to my entire
satisfaction." As indeed his course in the discharge of the important duties of the station
met the public satisfaction also.

Our relations with Great Britain at the time,

---

[1] Wolcott to Ames, Gibbs's *Administrations of Washington
and Adams,* vol. ii. p. 402.

also the adjourned questions with France, wore a threatening aspect, and called for prudent action to avert serious consequences. The new secretary of state addressed himself with characteristic energy, moderation, and firmness to the adjustment of these difficulties, and with good results. His instructions to Rufus King, our minister to the court of St. James, respecting the claims of British creditors and neutral rights, hold deservedly high rank among American state papers.

It was a difficult task in the discussion of these questions, with such jealous rivals as England and France, to preserve amicable relations with both; each party being watchful of any advantage the opposite side might gain in the negotiations. The pretension which those nations then put forth, that one nation may of right interfere in the affairs of another as independent as itself, though a postulate of the European system of that day, was not conceded by the United States, but was, on the contrary, firmly resisted. Thus Jay's treaty had been ratified in spite of the opposition and threats of France, and our negotiations with France were pushed to a successful issue notwithstanding the clamor of England. It was in this spirit that the American secretary of state wrote in a dispatch to Minister King: —

" The United States do not hold themselves in any degree responsible to France or to Great Britain for their negotiations with one or the other of those powers, but they are ready to make amicable and reasonable explanations to either. The aggressions, sometimes of one and sometimes of another belligerent power, have forced us to contemplate and prepare for war as a probable event. We have repelled, and we will continue to repel, injuries not doubtful in their nature, and hostilities not to be misunderstood. But this is a situation of necessity, not of choice ; it is one in which we are placed, not by our own acts, but by the acts of others, and which we will change as soon as the conduct of others will permit us to change it."

When the presidential election in 1800 had resulted in transferring the choice between Jefferson and Burr to the House of Representatives, Mr. Marshall was inclined to the opinion that the federal party should support the pretensions of the latter, though he viewed the alternative with great reluctance and regret. In the midst of these doubts and difficulties he received a letter from Alexander Hamilton, delineating the character of Burr, which seems to have shaken his predilection for that gentleman. It is in this connection a significant circumstance that he was induced to this change of mind by Hamilton's arguments. He wrote to Hamilton as follows : —

" Being no longer in the House of Representatives, and, consequently, being compelled by no duty to decide between them, my own mind had scarcely determined to which of these gentlemen the preference was due. To Mr. Jefferson, whose political character is better known than that of Mr. Burr, I have felt almost insuperable objections. His foreign prejudices seem to me totally to unfit him for the chief magistracy of a nation which cannot indulge those prejudices without sustaining deep and permanent injury.

" In addition to this solid and immovable objection, Mr. Jefferson appears to me to be a man who will embody himself with the House of Representatives, and, by weakening the office of President, he will increase his personal power. He will diminish his reponsibility, sap the fundamental principles of the government, and become the leader of that party which is about to constitute the majority of the legislature. . . . With these impressions concerning Mr. Jefferson, I was, in some degree, disposed to view with less apprehension any other characters, and to consider the alternative now offered us as a circumstance not to be entirely neglected.

" Your representation of Mr. Burr, with whom I am entirely unacquainted, shows that from him still greater danger than from Mr. Jefferson may be apprehended. Such a man as you describe is more to be feared, and may do more immediate if not greater mischief. Believing that you know him well and are impartial, my preference would certainly not be for him ; but I can take no part in this business. I cannot bring myself to aid Mr. Jefferson. Perhaps respect for myself should, in my present situation, deter me from using any influence — if indeed I possess any — in support of either gentleman. Although no consideration could induce me to be the secretary of state while there was a President whose political system I believed to be at variance with my own, yet this cannot be so well known to others, and it might be suspected that a desire to be well with the successful candidate had in some degree governed my conduct." [1]

In closing this sketch of Mr. Marshall as secretary of state, it is perhaps not improper to advert briefly to certain alleged transactions in his conduct of that department which, if true, would mark with some reproach the final hours of his administration, but against the truth of which his whole life is a pregnant protest.

It was while secretary of state, as we shall see in the succeeding chapter, that Mr. Marshall, on the 31st of January, 1801, was appointed Chief Justice of the United States, only a little more than one month before the expiration of the term of office of President Adams. He took the oath of office and his seat on the bench of the Supreme Court at the commencement of the next term, namely, on the 4th of February,

[1] Marshall to Hamilton, January, 1801. *Hamilton's Works*, vol. ii. p. 445.

1801, as the records of the court show. It was
at the special request of President Adams, by
a letter dated on the same day, that Mr. Marshall continued to act as secretary of state until
his successor should be appointed; or, to use the
language of the President's letter, "until ulte-
rior arrangements can be made." Again on
March 4, inauguration day, he was requested
by President Jefferson to perform the same duties for the like interval. His successor, Mr.
Madison, was appointed on the next day; but
Madison being absent, Mr. Levi Lincoln was
designated to perform the duties of the office
until the arrival of Mr. Madison. These dates
are suggestive and important, as they serve to
correct and disprove the misstatements referred
to, circulated by political opponents for party
purposes.

The story is, that late at night on the 3d of
March, President Adams was rapidly making
Federalist nominations to high official positions,
and sending them to the Senate for confirmation, and that Secretary Marshall was zealously
engaged in his office in signing them; that midnight overtook him still thus employed, when
Levi Lincoln, the in-coming attorney general
of the new government, walked into the secretary's office, with Mr. Jefferson's watch in his
hand, pointed to the hour of twelve, and thus

stopped the further progress of the not very reputable business. Many unsigned commissions, it was said, still lay on the table. Such conduct, it was alleged, bad enough in itself, was made worse by the pledge of generous forbearance which Mr. Jefferson had given, to the effect that there should be no interference with persons holding government positions when he should come into office.

In the absence of all proof, and without any authority being vouched to support the charge, we might have passed over the story without even pausing to give it a moment's consideration, for every intelligent man knows well that such an imputation would be contradicted by the whole tenor of Marshall's life, and would be justly regarded as the mere offspring of party malice or invention. But when a modern biographer [1] of cleverness and popularity, in relating the history of these times, ventures to impart credibility to the story and to narrate it in full, it deserves some notice and justifies a call for proof.

The foregoing unquestionable and easily provable facts certainly make out an overwhelming probability of the untruth of the charge. It is to the last degree improbable that Judge Marshall, being only the *locum tenens* of the post of

[1] James Parton in *Life of Jefferson,* pp. 585, 586.

secretary of state to prevent the lapse of the office, a secretary *ad interim* to prevent a vacancy, and with full employment at the time on the bench of the Supreme Court then in session, having, in his acceptance of the chief justiceship, stepped from the political arena to the strictly neutral ground of necessary exemption from all party ties and affiliations, should so far forget what was due to his own dignity and his official position as to descend from that lofty eyrie to the dust and discredit of a mere squabble for the spoils of office, in which he could have felt no particular interest.

Again, if this tale be true, the facts must have been known to Mr. Jefferson through Levi Lincoln, and would inevitably have incensed him with Marshall; so that it would have been to the last degree improbable, so improbable as to be almost incredible, that he should have sought out Marshall, and at the inauguration on the 4th of March should have taken the oath of office before him, when any other judge or magistrate would have been competent to act; and it is still more improbable and incredible that on that very day he should have invited Marshall to remain in his cabinet until a successor should be appointed! Moreover, Mr. Jefferson, we know, was never reluctant to give vent to his complaints and to record them, as his *Anas*

show, against those whom he supposed to stand
in his way; and no charge of this kind against
Marshall appears; though Jefferson did not like
Marshall, and found him, upon the bench, a serious obstacle in the way of Democratic policy.
Nay, he has left behind him a letter, in which
he bitterly denounces John Adams's appointment of the " midnight judges " and others to
office in the last hours of his administration,
without any censure on Secretary Marshall as
participating in the transaction, whom he certainly would not have spared, had he had any
ground to suspect him of complicity in this
darkling scene.

A curious anachronism is involved between
this "dramatic tale " as told by Mr. Parton
and Mr. Jefferson's reference to the same occasion, which serves further to disprove the whole
story. While the former fixes the midnight
hour for the " outrage on decency " complained
of, Mr. Jefferson limits the hour to nine o'clock
at night of the 3d of March, when the transactions were consummated ! Writing on the subject afterwards Jefferson says : " Mr. Adams
was making appointments, not for himself but
for his successor, until nine o'clock of the night
at twelve o'clock of which he was to go out of
office. This outrage on decency should not
have its effect except in the life appointments :

. . . as to the others I consider the nominations as nullities." The fact, if it occurred as nar-. rated by Parton, including the appearance even of Mr. Jefferson's own watch among the theatrical " properties," could not have been unknown to Jefferson, and was not likely to be set down by him with the palliation of three busy hours.

These facts, which are all patent, and most of which are of official record, afford such disproof of the statement referred to as to be conclusive. It is safe, therefore, to dismiss the story as unworthy of any credence whatever.

It was in this year, 1801, and soon after his retirement from the department of state, that the New Jersey College, better known as Princeton, conferred on General Marshall the degree of LL. D.

CHAPTER X.

THE appointment of John Marshall to the position of Chief Justice of the United States on the 31st of January, 1801, marks an epoch in the political and judicial history of the country. American jurisprudence, in many respects different from English jurisprudence, of which it was an offshoot rather than a reproduction, was then in its infancy; and American constitutional law was, of course and by necessity, a science quite unknown to the common law as well as to the British statutes in which American lawyers had been previously trained. The creation of a national government by the terms of a written paper was, as yet, a bold novelty, a brilliant but perilous experiment, made alarmingly complex by the establishment of collateral semi-sovereignties in the shape of the thirteen states. People might well be pardoned for feeling extreme anxiety and distrust when they contemplated the number, variety, and

11

difficulty of the questions which must arise to be determined by officers, who, however intelligent and honest, could yet have had no previous experience under a system so complex. The Constitution of the United States had sprung into birth amid popular discussions and debates as to the rights of man and the true principles of government almost as stormy as the long war just ended. Although that constitution had been adopted by the suffrage of a majority of the States of the confederation, yet its administration, at every step, was narrowly and jealously watched by a large proportion, possibly not a minority, of the whole people. These opponents almost hopefully predicted its speedy failure, and foretold, with something like a grim delight, the abundant evils and disasters which would follow in the wake of its overthrow. Many of them labored hard to fulfill their own gloomy prophecies. The machinery of the new government was not yet smoothly adjusted, and the friction incident to every new system grated harshly on the public sense. The popular apprehension of miscarriage and misfortune had become so sensitive that even Washington's patriotic, wise, and cautious administration was opposed with a vehemence altogether disproportioned to any adequate cause. This spirit surprised, at the time, thoughtful and considerate men, and the memory of its excesses even now excites the astonishment and indignation of succeeding generations. The presidency of John Adams, the pure patriot and honest statesman of the Revolutionary era, had fallen into great disfavor with the people, and the election of Thomas Jefferson, the head and leader of the opposition party, denoted a new strain about to be applied to the imperfectly developed powers of the government, through an entire change in the direction of public affairs.

It was at this crisis that Mr. Marshall was, by the wise choice of President Adams, called to the head of the judicial department. In this appointment the President, with far-reaching sagacity, departed from the natural order of precedence, which at that time favored the promotion of those already on the bench, whose judicial experience might be supposed to give them superior qualifications. Doubtless he was led to the selection of Mr. Marshall from the bar by an instinctive perception of a peculiar fitness in him for the place. If this was so, never, surely, was a more correct appreciation shown. If President Adams had left no other claims on the grateful remembrance of his countrymen than in giving to the public service this great magistrate, so pure and so wise, he would always have lived in that act, as a great benefactor of his country. The aged patriot survived long enough to see abundant proof of the soundness of his choice, and to rejoice in it.

In an unpublished account of a visit of Edward C. Marshall, the youngest son of Chief Justice Marshall, to the venerable ex-President, contained in a private letter addressed to Brooks Adams, Esq., Mr. Marshall says : —

" In the year 1825, I paid a visit to your greatgrandfather in Quincy. He gave me a most cordial reception, and grasping my hands told me that his gift of John Marshall to the people of the United States was the proudest act of his life. Some years after, in conversation with my father, he [my father] told me that the appointment was a great surprise to him, but afforded him the highest gratification, as, with his tastes, he preferred to be Chief Justice to being President." [1]

It is remarkable that when Mr. Marshall was called to the seat of Chief Justice of the United States he had never yet filled any judicial station. In this respect his appointment was a very bold step, for although he was

[1] For this original letter, and for other facilities in his work, the author is indebted to Mr. John Marshall of Markham, Va., the grandson, and to the Marshall family of Happy Creek, Warren County, Va., descendants of the Chief Justice.

known to be an able lawyer, it did not follow that he would, of necessity, make a great judge, or, still more, that he would be a competent leader of the bench. He was sure to be confronted in his new position by difficulties and embarrassments of the most formidable character. Besides being wholly without previous judicial experience, he had the peculiar task of reaching conclusions in matters wherein books and authorities could give him little aid, and of being required to solve questions in respect to which there were no precedents either in theory or practice. Like the sturdy pioneer of our western wilderness, he had to cleave his way through a pathless forest, with no guide but his instinctive resolution, and no help but the resources of his native genius and sagacity.

Such were the solidity and the clearness of his understanding, and especially such was his ready, almost intuitive perception of the principles of fundamental justice and right, which underlie the whole fabric of the law, that even on an originally slender foundation of legal acquirement he soon reared a structure which entitled him, in mature life, to the highest rank in his profession. The task which Marshall had to perform was the arduous one of construction; fortunately he had to a very striking degree the constructive faculty, a rare gift and certainly the highest form of intellectual ability which lawyers can ever use and display. He was a builder, from the very foundations, of a vast edifice by wholly new rules, under entirely novel exigencies, and for ends and purposes never before sought. It must be admitted that at no time of his forensic or judicial career was he remarkable for juridical learning. But he possessed that wonderful faculty of a sound discriminating judgment and a comprehensive sense of right, legal as well as moral, which was better than mere law reading. William Pinkney, of Maryland, after listening to several opinions rendered by him in the Supreme Court, said: " He was born to be the chief justice of any country in which he lived;" and it is within the memory of living witnesses and members of that bar that he was wont, at times, to say substantially in the conclusion of his masterly decisions: " These seem to me to be the conclusions to which we are conducted by the reason and spirit of the law. Brother Story will furnish the authorities." Of this peculiarity of his intellect Judge Story, so long and intimately associated with him, bears testimony.

" That he possessed an uncommon share of juridical learning would naturally be presumed from his large experience and inexhaustible diligence; yet it is due to truth as well as to his memory to declare that his juridical learning was not equal to that of many of the great masters of the profession, living or dead, at home or abroad. He yielded at once to their superiority of knowledge as well in the modern as in the ancient law. He adopted the notion of Lord Bacon, that 'Studies serve for delight, for ornament, and for ability' 'in the judgment and disposition of business.' The latter was his favorite object. Hence he read not to contradict and confute, not to believe and take for granted, not to find talk and discourse, but to weigh and consider."

He also followed another suggestion of that great man, that " Judges ought to be more learned than witty, more reverent than plausible, more advised than confident." The original bias as well as choice of his mind was to general principles and comprehensive views rather than to technical or recondite learning. He loved to expatiate upon the theory of equity, to elucidate the expansive doctrines of commercial jurisprudence, and to give a rational cast even to the most subtle dogmas of the common law. He was solicitous to hear arguments, and reluctant to decide causes without them, nor did any judge ever profit more by them. No matter whether the subject was new or old, familiar to his thoughts or remote from them, buried under a mass of obsolete learning or developed for the first time yesterday, whatever was its nature, he courted argument, nay he demanded it.

⌐ The Chief Justice, when appointed, had reached the age of forty-five.   William Wirt thus describes him : —

" The Chief Justice of the United States is in his person tall, meagre, emaciated; his muscles so relaxed as not only to disqualify him apparently for any vigorous exertion of body, but to destroy everything like harmony in his air and movements.   Indeed, in his whole appearance and demeanor, dress, attitudes, gesture, sitting, standing, or walking he is as far removed from the idolized graces of Lord Chesterfield as any other gentleman on earth.   His head and face are small in proportion to his height; his complexion swarthy; the muscles of his face, being relaxed, make him appear to be fifty years of age, nor can he be much younger.   His countenance has a faithful expression of great good humor and hilarity, while his black eyes, that unerring index, possess an irradiating spirit, which proclaims the imperial powers of the mind that sits enthroned within."

About the same period of his life, Mr. Story, afterwards Judge Story, then a member of the bar, who was in Washington to argue the case of Fletcher *v.* Peck in the Supreme Court, thus describes the Chief Justice, in a letter to a friend : —

"Marshall is of a tall, slender figure, not graceful or imposing, but erect and steady. His hair is black, his eyes small and twinkling, his forehead rather low, but his features are in general harmonious. His manners are plain, yet dignified, and an unaffected modesty diffuses itself through all his actions. His dress is very simple, yet neat. His language chaste, but hardly elegant. It does not flow rapidly, but it seldom wants precision. In conversation he is quite familiar, but is occasionally embarrassed by a hesitancy and drawling. His thoughts are always clear and ingenious, sometimes striking, and not often inconclusive.

" He possesses great subtlety of mind, but it is only occasionally exhibited. I love his laugh, it is too hearty for an intriguer ; and his good-temper and unwearied patience are equally agreeable on the bench and in the study. . . .

" He examines the intricacies of a subject with calm and persevering circumspection and unravels its mysteries with irresistible acuteness." [1]

" There is no man in the court that strikes me like Marshall," wrote Daniel Webster, then a member of Congress from New Hampshire. " I have never seen a man of whose intellect I had a higher opinion." [2]

Once, in allusion to the common expression of the Chief Justice, " It is admitted," Web-

---

[1] Story's *Life and Letters,* vol i. p. 166.

[2] *Private Correspondence of Daniel Webster,* vol. i. p. 243.

ster remarked to Judge Story, " When Judge
Marshall says, ' It is admitted,' sir, I am preparing for a bomb to burst over my head and
demolish all my points." [1]

The abilities of the new Chief Justice were
recognized by the profession and the public at
the time of his appointment, but the attractive
qualities of his heart and his kindly manners
soon caused respect and reverence to ripen into
affection. Perhaps no American citizen except
Washington ever conciliated so large a measure
of popularity and public esteem. He combined
in a remarkable degree those attributes of mind
and disposition which eminently fitted him for
his station and made him a great magistrate.

" His mind," in the words of an accomplished contemporary writer,[2] " is not very richly stored with
knowledge, but it is so creative, so well organized by
nature, or disciplined by early education and constant
habits of systematic thinking, that he embraces every
subject with the clearness and facility of one prepared by previous study to comprehend and explain
it. So perfect is his analysis that he extracts the
whole matter, — the kernel of inquiry, unbroken,
clean, and entire. In this process, such are the instinctive neatness and precision of his mind that no
superfluous thought or even word ever presents itself,

[1] Story's *Life and Letters*, vol. ii. p. 505.
[2] *Sketches and Essays of Public Characters*, by Francis W.
Gilmer.

and still he says everything that seems appropriate to the subject."

" It was matter of surprise," says Judge Story, " to see how easily he grasped the leading principles of a case and cleared it of all its accidental incumbrances ; how readily he evolved the true points of the controversy, even when it was manifest that he never before had caught even a glimpse of the learning upon which it depended. Perhaps no judge ever excelled him in the capacity to hold a legal proposition before the eyes of others in such various forms and colors. It seemed a pleasure to him to cast the darkest shades of objection over it, that he might show how they could be dissipated by a single glance of light. He would, by the most subtle analysis, resolve every argument into its ultimate principles ; and then, with a marvelous facility, apply them to the decision of the cause."

It is worthy of remark that perhaps no court has ever had the advantage of a more distinguished and able bar to practice in it than was the bar of the Supreme Court at the time when Marshall presided there. Of the thirteen original states, Massachusetts contributed the great names of Dexter and Webster, New York sent Hoffman, Wells, Ogden, Emmett, and Oakly ; Pennsylvania supplied Tilghman, Rawle, Ingersoll, Duponceau, Hopkinson, Sergeant, and Binney ; Maryland asserted a high place in the persons of William Pinkney and Robert Goodloe Harper; and Virginia was well represented by Wickham, Tazewell, Leigh, Edmund Randolph, Robert B. Taylor, Patton, the brilliant Wirt, and Walter Jones. The decisions of the Chief Justice may be said to bear the impress as well of the minds of these great lawyers as of his own.

In surveying the results of the labors of thirty-four years recorded in thirty-two volumes of reports, it is obvious that it was in the decision of cases involving international and constitutional law that the force and clearness of the Chief Justice's intellect shone most conspicuous. Such was the ready assent of his colleagues on the bench to his supremacy in the exposition of constitutional law, that in such causes a dissenting opinion was almost unknown. Having had occasion to discuss and thoroughly study the Constitution, both in the Virginia convention which adopted it and afterward in the legislature, he had preconceived opinions concerning it, as well as perfect familiarity with it. But in the hot contest waging between the friends of a strict and those of a liberal construction of its language, he wished to take no part. He stated that there should be neither a liberal nor a strict construction, but that the simple, natural, and usual meaning of its words and phrases should govern their in-

terpretation.[1] In the case of Gibbons *v.* Ogden,
in which he is called upon to define the true
rule of construction of the United States Constitution regarding the rights of the States and
the rights and powers of the general government, he studiously avoids each extreme, steer-
ing safely in the middle course. He lays down
his own rule thus clearly and definitely : —

" This instrument contains an enumeration of powers expressly granted by the people to their government. It has been said that these powers ought to
be construed strictly ; but why ought they to be so
construed ? Is there one sentence in the Constitution
which gives countenance to this rule ? In the last of
the enumerated powers, that which grants expressly
the means for carrying all others into execution, Congress is authorized to make all laws that shall be
necessary and proper for the purpose. But this
limitation on the means which may be used is not
extended to the powers which are conferred, nor is
there one sentence in the Constitution which has been
pointed out by the gentlemen of the bar, or which
we have been able to discern, that prescribes this
rule. We do not therefore think ourselves justified
in adopting it. What do gentlemen mean by a strict
construction ? If they contend only against that enlarged construction which would extend words beyond
their natural and obvious import, we might question

---

[1] Wheaton, vol. ix. p. 187.

the application of the term but should not controvert the principle. If they contend for that narrow construction which, in support of some theory not to be found in the Constitution, would deny to the government those powers which the words of the grant, as usually understood, import, and which are consistent with the general views and objects of the instrument; for that narrow construction which would cripple the government, and render it unequal to the objects for which it is declared to be instituted, and to which the powers given, as fairly understood, render it competent; then we cannot perceive the propriety of this strict construction, nor adopt it as a rule by which the Constitution is to be expounded."

And again, —

" Powerful and ingenious minds, taking as postulates that the powers expressly granted to the Union are to be contracted by construction into the narrowest possible compass, and that the original powers of the States are retained, if any possible construction will retain them, may, by a course of well digested but refined and metaphysical reasoning founded on these premises, explain away the Constitution of our country and leave it a magnificent structure indeed to look at, but totally unfit for use. They may so entangle and perplex the understanding as to obscure principles which were before thought quite plain, and induce doubts where, if the mind were to pursue its own course, none would be perceived. In such a case it is peculiarly necessary to recur to safe and fundamental principles, to sustain those principles, and when sustained to make them the tests of the arguments to be examined."

In another case — Ogden *v.* Saunders [1] — he expounds incidentally the rule which ought to be applied to the construction of the Constitution.

"To say," he observed, "that the intention of the instrument must prevail, that this intention must be collected from its words, that its words are to be understood in that sense in which they are generally used by those for whom the instrument was intended, that its provisions are neither to be restricted into insignificance, nor extended to objects not comprehended in them nor contemplated by its framers, is to repeat what has been already said more at large, and is all that can be necessary."

These are undoubtedly wise and sound views of the scope and powers of the federal government under the Constitution, which cannot be controverted. In view of our bitter experience of the evils of departing from them, exemplified in the disastrous and destructive civil war through which our country has so recently passed, it would seem that the language of the venerated Chief Justice was almost prophetic. Neither forcible nullification nor peaceable secession, claimed as legal and constitutional rem-

[1] Wheaton, vol. xii. p. 332.

edies for real or imaginary political wrongs, were to be found in the Constitution. They were the natural outcome of that narrow construction of the instrument which denied to the government those powers of self-assertion and self-preservation which were necessary not only to its purposes, but even to its existence.

Marshall's *dictum* that there must be neither a strict nor a liberal construction of the Constitution, but that the natural meaning of the words must govern, was undoubtedly sound and wise. The broad proposition was above criticism; it meant only that the language of the instrument should not be stretched or wrenched in any direction; and however politicians or even statesmen might feel, there was no other possible ground for a judge to take. Jefferson might regard it as a duty to make the Constitution as narrow and restricted as possible; Hamilton might feel that there was an actual obligation upon him to make it as broad and comprehensive as its words would admit. But Jefferson and Hamilton, in a different department of public life from Marshall, had duties and obligations correspondingly different from his. They might properly try to make the Constitution mean what it seemed to them for the public welfare that it should mean. Marshall could not consider any such matter; he had only to find and declare what it did mean, what its words actually and properly declared, not what they might possibly or desirably be supposed or construed to declare. This was the real force and the only real force of his fore-going assertion. As an abstract statement of his function it was impregnable.

But, as with most broad principles, the difficulty lay in the application of it to particular cases. The constitutional questions which came before Marshall chiefly took the form of whether or not the Constitution conferred some power or authority upon Congress, or upon the Executive. Then the Federalist lawyers tried to show how much the language could mean, and the anti-Federalist counsel sought to show how little it could mean, and each urged that public policy was upon his side. The decision must be yes or no ; the authority did or did not rest in the government. It was easy to talk about the natural and proper meaning of the words ; but after all it was the question at issue; did they (not *could* they) say yes, or did they (not *could* they) say no, to the special authority sought to be exercised.

Now it is one thing to be impartial and another to be colorless in mind. Judge Marshall was impartial and strongly possessed of the judicial instinct or faculty. But he was by no

12

means colorless. He could no more eliminate
from his mind an interest in public affairs, and
opinions as to the preferable forms of government and methods of administration, than he
could cut out and cast away his mind itself.
Believing that the Constitution intended to
create and did create a national government,
and having decided notions as to what such a
government must be able to do, he was subject
to a powerful though insensible influence to
find the existence of the required abilities in
the government. Thus when he was asked
what certain words meant, the meaning which
they bore to his mind would often be different
from the meaning which they bore to the mind
of a person differing from him in opinion concerning the subject to which the words related.
The meaning which the words had for him inevitably seemed their natural and proper meaning. Thus in all cases of doubt the decision
must reflect the complexion of his mind. It
cannot be denied, nor is it at all derogatory
to him, that this was the case. The great
majority of his decisions were in accordance
with Federalist principles of construction and
of policy. The Republicans all denounced him
as a Federalist, even of an extreme type. The
Federalists accepted him as one of themselves,
but of course considered that, as a clear-minded

and honest man, he could be nothing else. His very federalism was to them proof of his impartiality and sound judgment.

It is coming gradually to be conceded that the prevalence of the Federalist policy during the early years of our nationality was very fortunate for the country; that the party established a government neither too powerful nor too centralized; whereas the Republicans, if they had conquered the administration in the first plastic years, might have dangerously emasculated it. Marshall's decisions have always been regarded as wise and fortunate for the nation. No judge or lawyer enjoys a greater or a more deserved reputation as a constitutional jurist. Yet it is true that in many of the causes before him, — take for example the famous one involving the constitutionality of the United States Bank, — he could have given opposite decisions, had he been so minded, and as matter of *pure law* these opposite decisions might often have been just as good as those which he did give. Ploughing in fresh ground he could run his furrows in what direction he thought best, and could make them look straight and workmanlike. He had no rocks in the shape of authorities, no confusing undulations in collections of adjudications tending in one or another direction. He was making law; he had only to be logical and consistent in the manufacture. He made Federalist law in nine cases out of ten, and made it in strong, shapely fashion. A Republican judge, however, would have brought about a very different result, which, as we believe, would have been vastly less serviceable to the people, but of which the workmanship in a strictly professional and technical view might have been equally correct.

The difficulty of the task which Marshall had to perform must not be underrated by reason of this description. It may seem to the layman that it is a very easy matter to be a judge where one is, in a certain sense, equally free to decide arbitrarily in either the negative or the affirmative. The contrary is the case. To travel over a road paved with authorities and lined out by adjudications is a much simpler task than to cut a new road in a strange territory. Moderate learning, the aid of counsel's arguments, painstaking and cautious habits, a little subtlety of mind, and good technical training, will make a very reputable judge for the ordinary work of the bench. But to construct law, to frame in any department a system of jurisprudence, are tasks which call for an intellect of the highest order. The few judges who have performed such labors, Holt, Mansfield, Marshall, are the really great juridical lights.

It may seem that it was comparatively simple for Marshall, in any case of entirely novel complexion, to say, It is — or, It is not — within the Constitution. But to support the decision by an opinion professionally and technically satisfactory, framed in accordance with the spirit of English law, consonant with its fundamental principles, to make it really satisfactory as a judicial opinion and not to leave it either as a ruling or an argument, was a much more difficult undertaking, which none save lawyers can fully appreciate. To deliver many such opinions, which, though upon distinct questions, should yet so combine and harmonize as in conjunction to create a system of constitutional law, was an achievement to which few judges who have ever lived could prove competent. The legal cast of mind must exist in a rare degree; the judicial faculty, an intellectual gift far beyond mere impartiality, must have an extraordinary development; great mental reach and scope, much exceeding what is usually admired as clearness of mind, are indispensable. The judge who rears such a monument to his memory will never be forgotten; in the united domain of English and American jurisprudence there are not half a dozen such memorials; but not the least distinguished is that of Marshall.

It is impracticable so much as to mention
even all the important causes in which Marshall delivered the opinions. Yet a very few
may, with difficulty, be selected from the mass
for the purpose, at least, of showing his manner
of treatment, if nothing more.

The first case in which he had to deal with
a constitutional question involved the inquiry
as to the power and the duty of the court to
set aside an act of Congress because of its repugnance to the federal Constitution. This
was in Marbury *v.* Madison.[1] The case possesses a peculiar interest because the decision
was very distasteful to the President, and the
opinion of the court delivered by the Chief
Justice elicited a captious and very unbecom-
ing criticism from Mr. Jefferson. The facts
were as follows : —

President Adams, before the expiration of
his term of office, nominated Marbury to the
Senate as justice of the peace for the District
of Columbia. The nomination was confirmed
by the Senate. A commission was filled up,
signed by the President, and sealed with the
seal of the United States, but had not been
delivered when Mr. Jefferson succeeded to the
office. He, acting on the idea that the appointment was incomplete and void so long as

---

[1] Cranch's *Reports,* vol. i. p. 158.

the commission remained undelivered, counter-manded its issue. A petition for a mandamus was presented to the court by Marbury, re-quiring Mr. Madison, the secretary of state, to deliver it. The aid of the court was invoked on the ground that an act of Congress author-ized that court " to issue writs of mandamus, in cases warranted by the principles and usages of law, to any courts appointed by or persons holding office under the authority of the United States." Two questions here presented them-selves : —

I. Whether the authority thus given to the Supreme Court, by the said act, to issue writs of mandamus to public officers was warranted by the Constitution.

II. If not, whether the court was competent to declare void the act which undertook to con-fer the authority.

The court first considered whether Marbury had a right to the commission which he claimed, and they decided that he had ; that an ap-pointment is complete when the commission is signed by the President, and when the seal of the United States has been affixed to it ; and that to withhold such commission from an officer not removable at the will of the Exec-utive is violating a vested legal right.

As the legality of his conduct in directing

Mr. Madison to withhold the commission from Marbury was drawn in question, though in no offensive sense, Mr. Jefferson might be pardoned for feeling much interest in the result. He took the ground that the validity of a commission, like that of a deed, depends on its delivery. The court thought otherwise; but as they also held that they had no cognizance of the case, because the act of Congress conferring the power on them was in violation of the Constitution, Jefferson considered their opinion as to the legality of Marbury's claim gratuitous — "an *obiter* dissertation of the Chief Justice, and a perversion of the law." [1] The decision of the court, however, 'both on the question of jurisdiction and on its power and duty to declare an act of Congress to be unconstitutional and void has always commanded universal assent.

Marshall, Chief Justice, delivering the opinion of the court, said: —

" The Constitution vests the whole judicial power of the United States in one Supreme Court, and such inferior courts as Congress shall, from time to time, ordain and establish.

" In the distribution of this power it is declared that ' the Supreme Court shall have original jurisdiction in all cases affecting ambassadors, other pub-

[1] Jefferson's *Works,* vol. vii. p. 290.

lic ministers, and consuls, and those in which a State shall be a party. In all other cases the Supreme Court shall have appellate jurisdiction.' To enable this court, then, to issue a mandamus, it must be shown to be an exercise of appellate jurisdiction, or to be necessary to enable them to exercise appellate jurisdiction. It is the essential criterion of appellate jurisdiction that it revises and corrects the proceedings in a cause already instituted, and does not create that cause. Although, therefore, a mandamus may be directed to courts, yet to issue such a writ to an officer for the delivery of a paper is, in effect, the same as to sustain an original action for that paper, and, therefore, seems not to belong to appellate but to original jurisdiction. The authority, therefore, given to the Supreme Court, by the act establishing the judicial courts of the United States, to issue writs of mandamus to public officers, appears not to be warranted by the Constitution, and it becomes necessary to inquire whether a jurisdiction so conferred can be exercised.

"The question whether an act repugnant to the Constitution can become the law of the land is a question deeply interesting to the United States; but, happily, not of an intricacy proportioned to its interest. If an act of the legislature repugnant to the Constitution is void, does it, notwithstanding its invalidity, bind the courts and oblige them to give it effect? Or, in other words, though it be not a law, does it constitute a rule as operative as if it was a law? This would be to overthrow in fact what was established in theory; and would seem, at first view, an absurdity too gross to be insisted on. It shall, however, receive a more attentive consideration. It is emphatically the province and duty of the judicial department to .say what the law is. Those who apply the rule to particular cases must, of necessity, expound and interpret that rule. If two laws conflict with each other, the courts must decide on the operation of each. So, if a law be in opposition to the Constitution; if both the law and the Constitution apply to a particular case, so that the court must either decide that case conformably to the law disregarding the Constitution, or conformably to the Constitution disregarding the law, the court must determine which of these conflicting rules governs the case. This is of the very essence of judicial duty. If, then, the courts are to regard the Constitution, and the Constitution is superior to any ordinary act of the legislature, the Constitution, and not such ordinary act, must govern the case to which they both apply."

Subsequently and upon the same reasoning, in Fletcher *v.* Peck,[1] the court declared void an act of the State of Georgia. The legislature of this State had passed an act authorizing a patent to issue for a tract of land within its limits. After the patent had been granted a succeeding legislature repealed the act which authorized it. It was contended that the first

---

[1] Cranch's *Reports*, vol. vi. p. 87.

act was repugnant to the Constitution of Georgia ; that the legislature which passed it had been bribed or corrupted; and that it was not competent for one legislative body to restrain a succeeding legislature from repealing its acts.

Marshall, Chief Justice, delivered the opinion of the court.

"The question whether a law be void for its repugnancy to the Constitution is at all times a question of much delicacy, which ought seldom, if ever, to be decided in the affirmative in a doubtful case. The court, when impelled by duty to render such a judgment, would be unworthy of its station could it be unmindful of the solemn obligations which that station imposes. But it is not on slight implication and vague conjecture that the legislature is to be pronounced to have transcended its powers, and its acts to be considered as void. The opposition between the Constitution and the law should be such that the judge feels a clear and strong conviction of their incompatibility with each other. In this case the court can perceive no such opposition. In the Constitution of Georgia, adopted in the year 1789, the court can perceive no restriction on the legislative powers which inhibits the passage of the act of 1795. The court cannot say that, in passing that act, the legislature has transcended its powers and violated the Constitution.

"The case, as made out in the pleadings, is simply this. An individual who holds lands in the State of

Georgia, under a deed covenanting that the title of Georgia was in the grantor, brings an action of covenant upon this deed, and assigns as a breach that some of the members of the legislature were induced to vote in favor of the law which constituted the contract by being promised an interest in it, and that therefore the act is a mere nullity. This solemn question cannot be brought thus collaterally and incidentally before the court. It would be indecent in the extreme, upon a private contract between two individuals, to enter into an inquiry respecting the corruption of the sovereign power of a State. If the title be plainly deduced from a legislative act, which the legislature might constitutionally pass, if the act be clothed with all the requisite forms of law, a court, sitting as a court of law, cannot sustain a suit brought by one individual against another, founded on the allegation that the act is a nullity in consequence of the impure motives which influenced certain members of the legislature which passed the law.

" The principle asserted is, that one legislature is competent to repeal an act which a former legislature was competent to pass, and that one legislature cannot abridge the powers of a succeeding legislature. The correctness of this principle, so far as it respects general legislation, can never be controverted. But if an act be done under a law, a succeeding legislature cannot undo it. The past cannot be recalled by the most absolute power. Conveyances have been made, those conveyances have vested legal estates, and if those estates may be seized by the sovereign authority, still that they originally vested is a fact, and cannot cease to be a fact. When, then, a law is in its nature a contract, when absolute rights have vested under that contract, a repeal of the law cannot divest those rights. . . . The validity of this rescinding act, then, might be doubted, were Georgia a single sovereign power. But Georgia cannot be viewed as a single, unconnected, sovereign power, on whose legislature no other restrictions are imposed than may be found in its own Constitution. She is a part of a large empire ; she is a member of the American Union ; and that Union has a Constitution the supremacy of which all acknowledge, and which imposes limits to the legislatures of the several States, which none claim a right to pass. The Constitution of the United States declares that 'no State shall pass any bill of attainder, *ex post facto* law, or law impairing the obligation of contracts.'

" Does the case now under consideration come within this prohibitory section of the Constitution? In considering this very interesting question we immediately ask ourselves, What is a contract? Is a grant a contract? 'A contract executed is one in which the object of contract is performed ; and this,' says Blackstone, 'differs in nothing from a grant.' The contract between Georgia and the purchasers was executed by the grant. A contract executed, as well as one which is executory, contains obligations binding on the parties. A grant in its own nature amounts to an extinguishment of the right of the grantor, and implies a contract not to reassert that right. A party is, therefore, always estopped by his own grant. . . . If, under a fair construction of the Constitution, grants are comprehended under the term 'contracts,' is a grant from a State excluded from the operation of the provision? Is the clause to be considered as inhibiting the State from impairing the obligation of contracts between two individuals, but as excluding from that inhibition in contracts made with itself? The words themselves contain no such distinction. They are general, and are applicable to contracts of every description. Why, then, should violence be done to the natural meaning of words for the purpose of leaving to the legislature the power of seizing, for public use, the estate of an individual in the form of a law annulling the title in which he holds the estate? The court can perceive no sufficient grounds for making this distinction."

The case of Dartmouth College,[1] which involved the important question whether a grant of corporate powers by Congress is a contract, whose obligation the States are inhibited from impairing, attracted great attention at the time, by reason of some peculiar circumstances surrounding it, and to this day remains one of the most interesting and important causes which have ever arisen in the Supreme Court. The facts were these: A charter was granted to Dartmouth College in 1769 by the Crown, on

[1] Wheaton, vol. iv. p. 518.

the representation that property would be given
to the college, if chartered ; and after the charter was granted property was actually given.
In 1816 the legislature of New Hampshire
passed three acts amending the charter, which
amendments the trustees would not accept.
They resorted to the aid of the state courts,
where judgment was given against them ; then
they appealed their case to the Supreme Court.
Mr. Hopkinson and Mr. Webster appeared for
the college, and the other side was represented
by Mr. Wirt, then Attorney General of the
United States, and Mr. Holmes. Great interest was manifested in the speeches of Webster
and Wirt. Mr. Webster had argued the case
in the courts below. He was familiar with the
whole field of controversy. He was a graduate
of the college, and his feelings as a man no less
than his ambition as an advocate urged him to
the utmost exertion of his intellect. His speech
before the court consumed more than four
hours, and was marked by his usual characteristics, — great clearness of statement and much
force and precision in his reasoning. His argument was considered one of the greatest of his
forensic life. His noble peroration is familiar.
Towards the close of it, overcome by emotion,
the speaker proceeded with difficulty. Pausing
to recover his composure, and fixing his eye

on the Chief Justice, he said in that deep tone which so often thrilled the heart of an audience: "Sir, I know not how others may feel," glancing at the opposing counsel before him, "but for myself, when I see my Alma Mater surrounded, like Cæsar in the senate house, by those who are reiterating stab upon stab, I would not for this right hand have her turn to me and say, *Et tu quoque, mi fili.*" With this he sat down, leaving his whole audience profoundly moved.

The argument of Mr. Wirt, in support of the acts of the legislature amendatory of the college charter, was described as full, able, and eloquent.

The opinion of the court was delivered by Marshall, Chief Justice.

"This is plainly a contract to which the donors, the trustees, and the Crown, to whose rights and obligations New Hampshire succeeds, were the original parties. It is a contract made on a valuable consideration. It is a contract for the security and disposition of property. It is a contract on the faith of which real and personal estate has been conveyed to the corporation. It is then a contract within the letter of the Constitution, and within its spirit also. Unless the fact that the property is invested by the donors in trustees, for the promotion of religion and education, for the benefit of persons who are perpetually changing, although the objects remain the same, shall create a particular exception, taking this case out of the prohibition contained in the Constitution. On what safe and intelligible ground can this exception stand? There is no expression in the Constitution, no sentiment delivered by its contemporaneous expounders, which would justify us in making it. In the absence of all authority of this kind, is there, in the nature and reason of the case itself, that which would sustain a construction of the Constitution not warranted by its words? Are contracts of this description of a character to excite so little interest that we must exclude them from the provisions of the Constitution as being unworthy of the attention of those who framed the instrument, or does public policy so imperiously demand their remaining exposed to legislative alteration as to compel us, or rather permit us, to say that these words, which were introduced to give stability to contracts, and which, in their plain import, comprehend this contract, must yet be so construed as to exclude it?"

He then proceeded through a course of careful reasoning to give a negative answer to these questions, and hence the opinion of the court was that the charter constituted a contract whose obligation the legislature of New Hampshire had attempted to impair, and that this action of the legislature was repugnant to the Constitution of the United States, and consequently void.

13

The celebrated case of McCulloch *v.* The State of Maryland [1] involved the question of the constitutional power of Congress to incorporate a national bank, a question which had elicited warm discussions throughout the country almost from the adoption of the Constitution, and which unhappily had been allowed to force itself into the political arena.   It was insisted, on the one hand, that the Constitution conferred no authority on Congress to create a corporation, notwithstanding the clause conferring the power to make all laws that were necessary and proper to carry into effect the powers enumerated in the instrument; that these words meant only such laws as were absolutely and indispensably necessary, without which the powers conferred must be nugatory.   On the other hand, it was contended that in order to carry on its operations the government must act by officers and agents, and that in the choice of these it was not restricted to means which were only absolutely necessary, but might have recourse to such as were proper and necessary in the ordinary sense and meaning of these words.

The case grew out of the following facts: In April, 1816, Congress incorporated the Bank of the United States.   In 1817 a branch of this

[1] Wheaton, vol. iv. p. 316.

bank was established at Baltimore. In 1818 the legislature of Maryland passed a law to tax all banks or branches thereof situated in that State and not chartered by its legislature. The branch bank refused to pay this tax, and McCulloch, the cashier, was sued for it. Judgment was rendered against him in the Maryland courts, whence the case was carried before the Supreme Court, and the decision of that tribunal was looked for with great interest. The most distinguished counsel were engaged in the conduct and argument of the cause. Pinkney, Wirt, and Webster were of counsel for the Bank; Luther Martin, Hopkinson, and Walter Jones appeared for the State of Maryland. It is said that on this occasion Pinkney, who made the closing argument, delivered a speech of unrivaled splendor and power. In delivering the opinion, Marshall, Chief Justice, said : —

"Although among the enumerated powers of government we do not find the word Bank, or Incorporation, we find the great powers to lay and collect taxes, to borrow money, to regulate commerce, to declare and conduct a war, and to raise and support armies and navies. The sword and the purse, all the external relations, and no inconsiderable portion of the industry of the nation, are intrusted to its government. The power being given, it is the interest of the nation to facilitate its execution. It can never be their interest, and cannot be presumed to have been their intention, to clog and embarrass its execution by withholding the most appropriate means. Throughout this vast republic, from the St. Croix to the Gulf of Mexico, from the Atlantic to the Pacific, revenue is to be collected and expended, armies are to be marched and supported. . . . Is that construction of the Constitution to be preferred which would render these operations difficult, hazardous, and expensive? Can we adopt that construction, unless the words imperiously require it, which would impute to the framers of that instrument, when granting these powers for the public good, the intention of impeding their exercise, by withholding the choice of means? The government, which has a right to do an act, and has imposed on it the duty of performing that act, must, according to the dictates of reason, be allowed to select the means; and those who contend that it may not select any appropriate means, that one particular mode of effecting the object is excepted, take upon themselves to prove the exception. . . . But the Constitution of the United States has not left the right of Congress to employ the necessary means for the execution of the powers conferred on the government to general reasoning. To its enumeration of powers is added that of making ' all laws which shall be necessary and proper for carrying into execution the foregoing powers and all other powers vested by this Constitution in the government of the United States or any department thereof.'

To employ the means necessary to an end is generally understood as employing any means calculated
to produce the end, and not as being confined to
those single means without which the end would be
entirely unattainable. . . . The good sense of the
people has pronounced without hesitation that the
power of punishment appertains to sovereignty, and
may be exercised, whenever the sovereign has a right
to act, as incidental to his constitutional powers. It
is a means for carrying into execution all sovereign
powers, and may be used, although not indispensably
necessary. It is a right incidental to the power and
conducive to its beneficial exercise. If the word *necessary* means *needful, essential, requisite, conducive to,*
in order to let in the power of punishment for the
infraction of law, why is it not equally comprehensive, when required to authorize the use of means
which facilitate the execution of the powers of government, without the infliction of punishment?"

As to the other question, whether the Bank
or its branches may be taxed by the States, he
said : —

" That the power to tax involves the power to destroy ; that the power to destroy may defeat and
render useless the power to create ; that there is a
plain repugnance in conferring on one government a
power to control the' constitutional measures of another, which other, with respect to those very measures, is declared to be supreme over that which exerts
the control, are propositions not to be denied. If the

States may tax one instrument employed by the government in the execution of its powers, they may tax any and every other instrument. They may tax the mail; they may tax the mint; they may tax patent rights; they may tax the papers of the custom-house; they may tax judicial process; they may tax all the means employed by the government, to an excess which would defeat all the ends of government. This was not intended by the American people. They did not design to make their government dependent on the States."

The decision of the court, in harmony with this reasoning, was that Congress possessed the power to charter the Bank with branches in any of the States, and that such branches could not be taxed by state authority.

To these leading cases, in which the Supreme Court was called upon, at an early day, to expound and reconcile questions of apparent conflict between federal and state laws under the Constitution, we add another, which occasioned great interest at the time, and has since firmly established the rule of law.

In the case of Cohen *v.* State of Virginia, two very important questions were presented for adjudication; namely, whether the court could exercise jurisdiction, where one of the parties was a State and the other was a citizen of that State; and secondly, whether, in the exercise of its appellate jurisdiction, it could revise the judgment of a state court, in a case arising under the Constitution, laws, and treaties of the United States. The court held that it had jurisdiction in both cases.

The facts involved in the case were these: An act of Congress authorized the city of Washington to establish a lottery, and by virtue of the act the lottery was established. Cohen was indicted at Norfolk, Virginia, for selling tickets of this lottery, contrary to a law of Virginia prohibiting such sales. In the state court he claimed the protection of the act of Congress under which the lottery was established; but judgment being given against him, he sued out a writ of error to the Supreme Court of the United States. There the judgment of the state court was sustained; it being held that the lottery law did not control the laws of the States prohibiting the sale of the tickets. The chief interest of the case, however, depended on the question, whether the Supreme Court could take cognizance of it; and it is with reference to that point that the opinion of the court is quoted. Chief Justice Marshall said : —

" It [the Supreme Court] is authorized to decide all cases of every description arising under the Constitution or laws of the United States. From this general grant of jurisdiction no exception is made of those cases in which a State may be a party. When we consider the situation of the government of the Union and of a State in relation to each other, the nature of our Constitution, the subordination of the state governments to that Constitution, the great purpose for which jurisdiction over all cases arising under the Constitution and laws of the United States is confided to the judicial department, are we at liberty to insert in this general grant an exception of those cases in which a State may be a party? Will the spirit of the Constitution justify this attempt to control its words? We think it will not. We think a case arising under the Constitution or laws of the United States is cognizable in the courts of the Union, whoever may be the parties to that case. The laws must be executed by individuals acting within the several States. If these individuals may be exposed to penalties, and if the courts of the Union cannot correct the judgments by which these penalties may be enforced, the course of the government may be at any time arrested by the will of one of its members. Each member will possess a *veto* on the will of the whole.

" That the United States form, for many and for most important purposes, a single nation has not yet been denied. These States are constituent parts of the United States. They are members of one great empire, for some purposes sovereign, for some purposes subordinate. In a government so constituted is it unreasonable that the judicial power should be competent to give efficacy to the constitutional laws of the legislature? That department can decide on the validity of the Constitution or law of a State, if it be repugnant to the Constitution or to a law of the United States. Is it unreasonable that it should also be empowered to decide on the judgment of a state tribunal enforcing such unconstitutional law? Is it so very unreasonable as to furnish a justification for controlling the words of the Constitution? We think not. . . . The exercise of the appellate power over those judgments of the state tribunals which may contravene the Constitution or laws of the United States is, we believe, essential to the attainment of those objects."

CHAPTER XI.

1806–1807.

IT was before Chief Justice Marshall that Aaron Burr, late Vice-President of the United States, was tried in the Circuit Court of the United States held in Richmond, Virginia, at the spring term of 1807. Burr was indicted for the crime of high treason, in levying war against the United States, and for a misdemeanor in preparing a military expedition against Mexico, then a territory of the King of Spain, with whom the United States was at peace. This event was the most remarkable and imposing of any which up to that time had marked the judicial annals of our country.

Whatever may be thought of the guilt or innocence of the accused and of the real purpose of the organized expedition which was actually set on foot by him on the soil of the United States, whether it was designed to effect a dismemberment of the American Union or only to wrest Mexico from Spain, the boldness of

the enterprise, the ambition and ability of the
leader, and the high rank and station of its alleged friends and promoters invested the project with extraordinary interest. Burr had
lately been a candidate for the Presidency of
the United States, and had come within one
electoral vote of being chosen. After a long
struggle, which it is not necessary here to
describe, Mr. Jefferson was elected President,
and Burr became the Vice-President, and as
president of the Senate he had so acquitted
himself as to add to his already high reputation. He stood well as a soldier by reason of
his services in the war for independence; and
he was widely known as a successful and able
lawyer. His conception, however, of the ethics
of his practice may be inferred from his defi-
nition of law, namely, " Whatever is boldly
asserted and plausibly maintained." In short,
in all the aspects of his public character he was
astute, able, and accomplished. Although of
small stature, he was remarkable in public life
for the commanding dignity of his manners and
his eloquent oratory, and in private, for an ease
and gracefulness of demeanor which attracted
the regards of men and dazzled and captivated
the other sex. A contemporary historian [1] thus
describes him : " He was brave, affable, munif-

[1] Safford, in his *Life of Blennerhassett*, pp. 71-182.

icent, of indomitable energy, of signal perseverance. In his own person he combined two
opposite natures. He was studious, but insinu-
ating; dignified, yet seductive; success did not
intoxicate, nor reverse dismay him. On the
other hand, he was profligate in morals, public
and private; selfish and artful — a master in
dissimulation, treacherous, cold-hearted, subtle,
intriguing, full of promise, a skeptic in honesty,
a scorner of all things noble and good, from
whom good men shrank in mistrust as from
a cold and glittering serpent." His duel with
Hamilton and its fatal end occurred on the 11th
of July, 1804, while he was Vice-President, and
proved the fruitful source of all the subsequent
calamities, social, political, and personal, which
marked him in after life as a doomed man, in
spite of his gifts and accomplishments. The
Federalists hated him for slaying their great
leader, and the Republicans could not approve
the manner of it, while they were further sus-
picious and incensed against him by reason of
warm and unfair competition with Mr. Jefferson for the Presidency. Burr, thus disowned
and disliked by his former associates in New
Jersey and New York especially, where indictments were still pending against him, began
naturally to regard himself as without home or
country, and resolved to seek another sphere in

which he should find new ties and a free scope for that restless ambition, which was the consuming fever of his life. This opportunity seemed to open before him in the almost belligerent relations now existing between Spain and the United States, growing out of the frequent incursions and hostile collisions between the citizens of these bordering territories, — the "border ruffians" of that day, — and stimulated by the ardent desire of the Americans to drive Spain from all foothold on this continent, and to get possession of the rich and attractive provinces of Mexico. The brilliantly successful career of Napoleon Bonaparte in Europe, mounting then to the pinnacle of fame by the splendor of his genius in civil and military achievement, was generally supposed to fire Burr's ambition, and feed the dream of romance which seemed to invite him to imitate such a career on the broad field of this Western Continent. To invade Mexico, and, like Cortes and his Castilians of old, to enrich themselves with wealth and booty and, in splendid luxury, to "revel in the halls of the Montezumas," seemed a feasible scheme to bold and reckless men. Even some who had wealth and high social position were induced to contribute of their means to the military chest of a leader who had a singular power of attracting men.

In pursuance of his plans, which seemed all to point to the invasion and conquest of Mexico, Burr, with characteristic energy, set out in the spring of 1805 to the western country on a tour of inspection and preparation. He was indefatigable in pushing forward his schemes. The war with Spain, apparently imminent, might enable him to proceed without a violation of laws or treaties. The western men, in their · usual adventurous spirit, were ready to join in ·an enterprise which promised such rich rewards, and which might, in due time, be openly favored by the national government. They so incited Burr that, although the probability of war between Spain and the United States began to fade away, yet he none the less zealously pushed on his preparations. He contracted for the construction on the Ohio River of a large number of transports for his "free companions," and designated Blennerhassett's Island, in the Ohio River, and within the jurisdiction of the State of Virginia, as a place of rendezvous for his eastern followers, and as the main depot of stores and supplies. Here accordingly was actually assembled a force of some thirty or forty men, the nucleus of his future army, who came armed with guns and pistols, which were worn, according to the custom of that country, by all citizens when they went from home. To provide for the contingency of the failure of his Mexican project, and as an alternative refuge, Burr bought four hundred thousand acres of land on the banks of the Wichita River in Texas. This region he proposed to maintain and for-.tify. Thus he was enabled to offer his followers the certainty of homes and rich lands, and to afford color to the pretension that his expedition was an agricultural and commercial enterprise, and therefore, of course, peaceful.

About this time Colonel Swartwout of New . York, who seems to have been Burr's chief of staff, arrived in the camp of General Wilkinson at Natchez, in Mississippi, bearing a letter in cipher from Burr to Wilkinson, in which Burr disclosed the particulars of the pending movement down the Ohio and Mississippi *en route* to New Orleans and thence to Mexico. Wilkinson and Burr had been comrades in the Revolutionary War, and had continued intimate and confidential friends. Burr had been Wilkinson's guest on his recent visit to the West, and was supposed to have conferred with him fully as to his projects. At least from the tenor of this cipher and other letters it appeared that he believed that he had secured Wilkinson's hearty coöperation. Wilkinson was at that time commander - in - chief of the United States army and military governor of the newly-acquired territory of Louisiana. The letter, which was long, contained the following paragraphs: —

"I, Aaron Burr, have obtained funds and have actually commenced the enterprise. . . . It will be a host of choice spirits. Wilkinson shall be second to Burr only. . . . Wilkinson shall dictate the rank and promotion of his officers. Burr will proceed westward by the first of August, nevermore to return. . . . Send forth an intelligent and confidential friend with whom Burr may confer. He shall return immediately with further interesting details. This is essential to concert and harmony of movement. . . .

"Burr's plan is . . . to be at Natchez between the 5th and 15th of December, there to meet Wilkinson. . . . Draw on Burr for all expenses, etc. The people of the country to which we are going are prepared to receive us. Their agents, now with Burr, say that if we will protect their religion and will not subject them to a foreign power, in three weeks all will be settled."

Wilkinson was greatly agitated by this letter, and seemed at first to hesitate as to his line of conduct. He had actually written and dispatched a letter to Burr, in which he was suspected of having promised an active, even personal coöperation in the enterprise. But, on second thought, he personally pursued and overtook the messenger, and intercepted and destroyed the letter. He then resolved to disclose and denounce the whole scheme to the government, denominating it a treasonable conspiracy to dismember the Union. Accordingly he forthwith sent one of his officers with the letter from Burr, duly interpreted from the cipher, accompanied by his own affidavit alleging Burr's guilt. These he sent directly to President Jefferson. They were delivered on the 25th of November. Then came the explosion. On the 27th of November the President issued his proclamation denouncing the scheme of conspiracy, and sent it on the wings of the wind, filling the country with consternation and alarm, in consequence of the general belief that the conspiracy extended from one end of the Union to the other. It was remarkable, however, that Burr's name was not mentioned, either in Wilkinson's dispatch or Jefferson's proclamation. Wilkinson indeed expressly, though falsely, declared that he did not know who was the prime mover of the conspiracy. By some means, it was soon after reported and known that it was an expedition of Colonel Burr against which the proclamation was leveled.

Wilkinson immediately seized Swartwout, Bollman, Ogden, and General Adair of Kentucky, as emissaries of Burr, and sent them under guard to Washington. A large reward

14

was offered for the arrest of Burr, who thereupon voluntarily came forward before the
United States courts and demanded a trial.
But no judge would commit him and no grand
jury would indict him, there being no evidence
of treasonable designs. He resolved, however,
to make his way to Pensacola, where he hoped
to meet a British man - of - war on which he
might take refuge.   In this effort he was arrested in Alabama by Major Perkins and hurried forward to Virginia under a small military
escort, without being offered any opportunity
of bringing his case before the courts, which
had, so far, afforded him immunity. He arrived,
in this way, at Richmond on the 26th of March,
1807, and was taken to the Eagle Hotel, still
under guard, and brought before Chief Justice
Marshall for examination preliminary to commitment, which was strenuously opposed by
Burr and his counsel.   After an examination
and arguments, which consumed three days, the
Chief Justice decided to commit the prisoner on
the charge of misdemeanor for having set on
foot a military expedition against Mexico, then
part of the dominions of the King of Spain,
with whom the United States was at peace.
The charge of high treason was reserved for
investigation by the grand jury.   Thus Burr
was freed from any immediate risk of imprison-

ment, and being entitled to bail, five gentlemen
of Richmond gave bail bonds in the sum of ten
thousand dollars for his appearance at the ensuing May term of the United States court;
whereupon he was discharged from custody.

On the opening of the court on the 22d of
May, 1807, the accused promptly appeared, attended by his counsel. These were Edmund
Randolph, a learned, experienced, and able lawyer, who had been Attorney General and Secretary of State under Washington, and Governor
and Attorney General of Virginia; John Wickham, a man of learning, wit, eloquence, logic,
and sarcasm, of a fine presence and persuasive
manner, perhaps the ablest lawyer then prac-
ticing at the Richmond bar; Benjamin Botts,
though a young man, already distinguished;
Charles Lee, formerly Attorney General of
the United States, and John Baker, familiarly
called "Jack" Baker, a useful man in such a
position, and a popular favorite on account of
his social qualities. These were supplemented,
later on in the trial, by Luther Martin of Maryland. Burr himself, however, was undoubtedly
the leader in the defense. His long and successful practice at the bar had made him perfectly at home in a court-room and such was
his self-possession, his calm dignity, and his
immovable composure that he never lost his

temper, nor was betrayed into mistakes. His speeches were short, but concise, and always to the point, and with the law on his side, and before a firm and fearless judge, he was equal to all the demands of the situation. Richmond, then a town of six thousand inhabitants, was crowded with visitors. Throngs of citizens, not only from Virginia, but from other States, were drawn thither by the celebrity of the occasion, and to witness the opening scenes of the most noteworthy trial which had yet marked the history of the Republic. Including lawyers from abroad, jurymen, and witnesses, it was estimated that not less than two hundred persons were in Richmond who had some official connection with the trial. The government, as prosecutor, was ably represented by George Hay, United States District Attorney; Alexander McCrae, an experienced and able lawyer of the Richmond bar, then Lieutenant-Governor of the State; and, on the special retainer of President Jefferson, by the gifted, accomplished, and eloquent William Wirt, then rising to the zenith of forensic fame. The court consisted of two judges; John Marshall, Chief Justice of the Supreme Court of the United States; and Cyrus Griffin, Judge of the District Court of Virginia.

When the grand jury were called, before

whom the indictment was to be laid, it soon
became evident that there had been a very extensive prejudgment of the case in the public
mind; for almost all the jurors, on being inter-
rogated, admitted that the proclamations of the
President and the depositions of General Eaton
and General Wilkinson had strongly impressed
them against the prisoner. The panel of the
grand jury which had been returned by the
marshal presented a list of the most intelligent, upright, and honorable citizens of the
State. No grand jury was ever convened in Virginia or elsewhere, composed of men of superior character and intelligence. After a very
thorough sifting of the original panel, and the
selection of substitutes for those who had been
withdrawn or excused, the requisite number
was at last obtained and sworn. John Randolph of Roanoke, then in the prime of his
powers, in spite of his request to be excused,
was made the foreman.

Although so long an interval as two months
had elapsed between the examination of Burr
before the Chief Justice at Richmond in the
preceding month of March and the meeting of
the court on the 22d of May, it was found that
little progress could be made in the trial until
the arrival of General Wilkinson, the chief
government witness, then in New Orleans. He

had been summoned, but did not present himself until the twenty-fourth day of the term.
During this interval several motions preliminary to the trial were made, and argued before
the court. One was presented by Colonel Burr
himself, asking the court to instruct the grand
jury as to the rule of admissibility of evidence
before them. Another was by Mr. Hay, the
district attorney, to commit the prisoner to
close custody to answer the charge of treason
now preferred in the indictment prepared for
the grand jury. On these motions the court delivered brief opinions overruling both. Referring to Hay's motion to commit the prisoner to
jail without bail on the charge of treason, the
court held that the charge could not be entertained except on proof, in the first instance,
that war had been actually levied, and that
some overt act of treason had been actually
committed by the prisoner; that treason was
declared in the Constitution " To consist only
in levying war against the United States, or in
adhering to their enemies, giving them aid and
comfort; " also, " that no person shall be convicted of treason, unless on the testimony of two
witnesses to the same overt act, or on confession in open court." It was fortunate for Colonel Burr, and for the cause of law and public
justice as well, that the American people had

oeen warned by the fate of so many martyrs and patriots, who had perished innocently on the scaffold in consequence of loose charges and vague definitions of treason made by the courts under the unwritten law of former times, and that, thus admonished, they had distinctly enacted in the Constitution that the crime should consist only in acts, and not in intentions and designs. The temper and aim of Marshall in the conduct of the cause appear in his own words : —

" That this court," said he, " dares not usurp power is most true. That this court does not shrink from its duty is not less true. No man is desirous of placing himself in a disagreeable situation. No man is desirous of becoming the peculiar subject of calumny. No man, might he let the bitter cup pass from him without reproach, would drain it to the bottom. But if he has no choice in the case, if there is no alternative presented to him but a dereliction of duty or the opprobrium of those who are denominated the world, he merits the contempt as well as the indignation of his country, who can hesitate which to embrace."

He did not mean to accept the judgment of the prejudiced public as the judgment of his court.

It was also in this stage of the case, while the court was awaiting the coming of General

Wilkinson, who was expected daily, that Colonel Burr, alleging that he had exhausted other means to procure certain papers which he deemed material for his defense, and which were in the possession, or under control of the executive department at Washington, copies of which had been refused him, moved the court for a *subpœna duces tecum*, to be directed to the United States marshal, commanding him to summon Thomas Jefferson, President of the United States, to appear before the court and bring with him, according to the exigency of the precept, the papers desired and designated in the prisoner's affidavit filed, especially the letter of General Wilkinson to the President, dated the 21st of October, 1806, and addressed directly to him. This motion was vehemently opposed by the counsel for the government, who alleged that it was wholly unnecessary, without any precedent, inconsistent with the President's official position and duties, and that it only tended, if it was not deliberately designed, to disparage and affront him. It elicited a warm discussion before the court, which consumed several days. After full argument, the Chief Justice delivered the opinion sustaining the motion. Some extracts from this opinion will develop the reasoning on which his conclusion rested.

"This point being disposed of, it remains," he said, "to inquire whether a *subpœna duces tecum* can be directed to the President of the United States, and whether it ought to be directed in this case?

"This question originally consisted of two parts. It was at first doubted whether a subpœna could issue in any case to the chief magistrate of the nation; and if it could, whether that subpœna could do more than direct his personal attendance; whether it could direct him to bring with him a paper which was to constitute the gist of his testimony. While the argument was opening, the attorney for the United States avowed his opinion that a general subpœna might issue to the President, but not a *subpœna duces tecum*. This terminated the argument on that part of the question. . . .

"In the provisions of the Constitution and of the statute which give to the accused a right to the compulsory process of the court, there is no exception whatever. The obligation therefore of those provisions is general, and it would seem that no person could claim an exemption from them but one who would not be a witness. At any rate, if an exception to the general rule exist, it must be looked for in the law of evidence. The exceptions furnished by the law of evidence (with one only reservation), so far as they are personal, are of those only whose testimony could not be received. The single reservation alluded to is the case of the King. Although he may perhaps give testimony, it is said to be incompatible with his dignity to appear under the process of the court. Of

the many points of difference which exist between the
first magistrate in England and the first magistrate
in the United States, in respect to the personal dignity conferred on them by the constitutions of their
respective nations, the court will only select two.

" It is a principle of the English Constitution that
the King can do no wrong, that no blame can be imputed to him, that he cannot be named in debate.

" By the Constitution of the United States, the
President, as well as every officer of the government,
may be impeached and may be removed from office
for high crimes and misdemeanors.

" By the Constitution of Great Britain, the crown
is hereditary and the monarch can never be a subject.

" By that of the United States, the President is
elected from the mass of the people; and, on the expiration of the time for which he is elected, returns
to the mass of the people again.

" How essentially this difference of circumstances
must vary the policy of the laws of the two countries,
in reference to the personal dignity of the chief Executive, will be perceived by every person. In this
respect, the first magistrate of the Union may more
properly be likened to the first magistrate of a State;
at any rate, under the former confederation. And it
is not known ever to have been doubted but that the
chief magistrate of a State might be served with a
subpœna ad testificandum.

" If in any court of the United States it has ever
been decided that a subpœna cannot issue to the
President, that decision is unknown to this court.

"If upon any principle the President could be construed to stand exempt from the general provisions
of the Constitution, it would be because his duties as
chief magistrate demand his whole time for national
objects.

"But it is apparent that this demand is not unremitting; and if it should exist at the time when his
attendance on the court is required, it would be sworn
on the return of the subpœna, and would rather constitute a reason for not obeying the process of the
court, than a reason against its being issued. . . . It
cannot be denied, that to issue a subpœna to a person filling the exalted station of chief magistrate
is a duty which would be dispensed with much more
cheerfully than it would be performed. But if it be
a duty, the court can have no choice in the case. . . .

"If, then, as is admitted by the counsel for the
United States, a subpœna may issue to the President, the accused is entitled to it, of course; and
whatever difference may exist with respect to the
power to compel the same obedience to the process
as if it had been directed to a private citizen, there
exists no difference with respect to the right to obtain it. The guard furnished to this high officer to
protect him from being harassed by vexatious and
unnecessary subpœnas is to be looked for in the conduct of the court, after those subpœnas had issued, not
in any circumstance which is to precede their being
issued. If in being summoned to give his personal
attendance to testify the law does not discriminate
between the President and a private citizen, what

foundation is there for the opinion, that this difference is created by the circumstance that his testimony depends on a paper in his possession, not on facts which have come to his knowledge otherwise than by writing? The court can perceive no foundation for such an opinion. The propriety of introducing any paper into a case as testimony must depend on the character of the paper, not on the character of the person who holds it. A *subpœna duces tecum*, then, may issue to any person to whom an ordinary subpœna may issue, directing him to bring any paper of which the party praying has the right to avail himself as testimony, if, indeed, that be the necessary process of obtaining such paper.

" When this subject was suddenly introduced, the court felt some doubt concerning the propriety of directing a subpœna to the chief magistrate, and some doubt also concerning the propriety of directing any paper in his possession, not public in its nature, to be exhibited in court. The impression that the questions which might arise, in consequence of such process, were more proper for discussion on the return of the process than on its issuing, was then strong on the minds of the judges; but the circumspection with which they would take any step which would in any manner relate to that high personage prevented their yielding readily to those impressions, and induced the request that those points, if not admitted, might be argued. The result of that argument is a confirmation of the impression originally entertained. The court can perceive no legal objection to issuing a *subpœna duces tecum* to any person whomsoever, provided the case be such as to justify the process. . . .

" The court would not lend its aid to motions obviously designed to manifest disrespect to the government; but the court has no right to refuse its aid to motions for papers, to which the accused may be entitled, and which may be material in his defense. . . .

" Much has been said about the disrespect to the chief magistrate which is implied by this motion, and by such a decision of it as the law is believed to require.

" These observations will be very truly answered by the declaration that this court feels many, perhaps peculiar motives, for manifesting as guarded a respect for the chief magistrate of the Union as is compatible with its official duties. To go beyond these would exhibit a conduct which should deserve some other appellation than the term respect.

" It is not for the court to anticipate the event of the present prosecution. Should it terminate, as is expected, on the part of the United States, all those who are concerned in it would certainly regret that a paper, which the accused believed to be essential to his defense, which may, for aught that now appears, *be* essential, had been withheld from him. I will not say that this circumstance would in any degree tarnish the reputation of the government, but I will say that it would justly tarnish the reputation of the court which had given its sanction to its being withheld. Might I be permitted to utter one sentiment with respect to myself, it would be to deplore most earnestly the occasion which should compel me to look back on any part of my official conduct with so much self-reproach as I should feel, could I declare, on the information now possessed, that the accused is not entitled to the letter in question, if it should be really important to him." [1]

We have been led to present so much of the ruling of the Chief Justice as will suffice to inform the reader of the ground of his conclusion, because, at the time, this ruling was bitterly arraigned and some modern authors have warmly dissented from it. Probably many of these critics have only followed the authority of President Jefferson, who had the bad taste and bad temper to denounce the opinion as an offensive trespass on the executive department of the government.

Mr. Parton tells us that Mr. Jefferson was disgusted with the motion, disgusted with the debate, and disgusted with the decision. [2] "Shall we move," Jefferson wrote to Mr. Hay, "to commit Luther Martin as *particeps criminis* with Burr? Grayball will fix upon him misprision of treason, at least; and, at any rate, his evidence will put down this unprincipled and impudent federal bull-dog, and add another

[1] *Burr's Trial*, vol. i. pp. 182, 183, 187, 188.
[2] Parton's *Life of Burr*, p. 474.

proof that the most clamorous defenders of Burr are all his accomplices. It will explain why Luther Martin flew so hastily to the 'aid of his honorable friend,' abandoning his clients and their property during a session of a principal court of Maryland, — now filled, as I am told, with the clamors and ruin of his clients." The indignant President promptly and emphatically denied the power of the court to require his attendance as a witness. " The Constitution," he wrote, "enjoins the President's agency in the concerns of six millions of people. Is the law paramount to this, which calls on him on behalf of a single one ? Let us apply the judge's own doctrine to the case of himself and his brethren. The sheriff of Henrico — Judge Marshall's residence — summons him from the bench to quell a riot somewhere in his county. The federal judge is by the general law a part of the *posse* of the state sheriff. Would the judge abandon major duties to perform lesser ones ? "

This letter shows the personal *animus* that inspired Mr. Jefferson's active interest in the trial at Richmond. It shows who was the real prosecutor of the prisoner, and who stimulated the zeal and the eloquence of those who were conducting the prosecution. It seems, from a careful inspection of the court's opinion, that

Chief Justice Marshall's plain duty, under the Constitution and the laws of the land, was to direct the *subpœna duces tecum* to issue, and to leave to the President on his part, as a coördinate branch of the government, the option of obeying the precept or of setting forth, in response to the process, the reasons for his failure or refusal to do so, of the sufficiency of which he must ultimately be, of necessity, the sole judge; for it was not supposed that any authority could *compel* his attendance. The opinion expressly declared that it would be only on the return of the process that questions might arise affecting its enforcement by any means in the power of the court; as to which, however, the court for the present declined to express any opinion as *coram non judice.* This essential part of the opinion the President, in his haste to condemn the court, seems to have wholly overlooked.

This ruling of the Chief Justice, it should be observed, seems to have been in harmony to this day with the practice which prevails in the legislative department, in calls which Congress may make, by resolution, on the President to furnish papers, documents, etc., in the executive departments, for their information. Such calls are always qualified by the *proviso* that the communication of the same be not, in his opinion, incompatible with the public interest. But the similarity is in spirit only; for the calls of Congress are requests, whereas the subpœna is in terms an *order;* and indeed a chief criticism was that the court put itself in a false position by issuing an *order* which it would probably be wholly incompetent to enforce.

The subpœna was sent accordingly, and in a few days the designated papers were transmitted to the court through the district attorney, and were used by the prisoner on his trial.

General Wilkinson, having at length arrived, was sent before the grand jury, who, after several days' deliberation and after examination of many witnesses, appeared in court and found "a true bill" on each of the indictments. The prisoner was then ordered into close custody, and the jail of the city proving to be an unhealthy asylum, he was soon, on the offer of the governor to the court, furnished with more suitable rooms at the State Penitentiary, to which his counsel and visiting friends had free access.

At length, after fourteen days spent in efforts to secure an impartial jury, and many challenges and much and able discussion as to their eligibility, a petit jury of twelve good men was chosen. The prisoner pleaded not guilty.

15

Early in the trial the prisoner's counsel moved the court to instruct the jury as to the law of treason and as to the preliminary proof of the overt act, in order to limit or exclude irrelevant testimony. After examination of many witnesses and full argument of counsel the Chief Justice expounded the law in these terms:—

"The whole treason laid in this indictment is the levying of war on Blennerhassett's Island; the whole question to which the inquiry of the court is now directed is whether the prisoner was legally present at that fact. I say this is the whole question, because the prisoner can only be convicted on the overt act laid in the indictment. With respect to this prosecution it is as if no other overt act existed. If other overt acts can be inquired into, it is for the sole purpose of proving the particular fact charged; it is as evidence of the crime consisting of this particular fact, not as establishing the general crime by a distinct fact. If the assemblage on Blennerhassett's Island was an assemblage in force, was a military assemblage, in a condition to make war and having a treasonable object, it was in fact a levying of war, and consequently treason. But, as the accused was not present and performing a part as charged, evidence of his acts elsewhere was irrelevant. In other words, the indictment charged him with actually levying war on Blennerhassett's Island, and therefore could not be supported by evidence which showed that he was actually absent from the scene of action

In short, that the government could not state one case and prove a very different one, or charge the prisoner with aiding in one transaction and prove him to be actually employed in another. If the prisoner advised, procured, or commanded the treasonable act, though this might not amount to treason under the Constitution of the United States, yet the indictment should have charged him with what he actually did, and the evidence should conform to the charge. . . . An assemblage, to constitute an actual levying of war, should be an assemblage with such force as to justify the opinion that they met for the purpose. Why is an assemblage absolutely required? Is it not to judge, in some measure, of the end by the proportion which the means bear to the end? Why is it that a single armed individual entering a boat and sailing down the Ohio for the avowed purpose of attacking New Orleans could not be said to levy war? Is it not that he is apparently not in a condition to levy war? If this be so, ought not the assemblage to furnish some evidence of its intention and capacity to levy war, before it can amount to levying war?"

As to the point made by the prosecution, that the accused, though personally absent, was constructively present, and must, therefore, be held responsible, the court said : —

"If the accused, though he had not arrived in the island, had taken a position near enough to coöperate with those on the island, to assist them in any act of hostility, or to aid them if attacked, he then might have been constructively present, and this would have been a mixed question of law and fact for the jury, with the aid of the court, to decide. . . . It is then the opinion of the court that this indictment can be supported only by testimony which proves the accused to have been actually or constructively present when the assemblage took place on Blennerhassett's Island, or by the admission of the doctrine that he who procures an act may be indicted as having performed that act. It is further the opinion of the court that there is no testimony whatever which tends to prove that the accused was actually or constructively present, when that assemblage did take place. Indeed the contrary is most apparent. With respect to admitting proof of procurement to establish a charge of actual presence, the court is of opinion that if this be admissible in England on an indictment for levying war, which is far from being conceded, it is admissible only by virtue of the operation of the common law upon the statute, and therefore is not admissible in this country unless by virtue of a similar operation; a point far from being established, but on which, for the present, no opinion is given. If, however, this point be established, still the procurement must be proved in the same manner and by the same kind of testimony which would be required to prove actual presence. If those who perpetrated the fact be not traitors, he who advised the fact cannot be a traitor. . . . His guilt, therefore, depends on theirs, and their guilt cannot be legally established in a prosecution against him. Now an assemblage on Blennerhassett's Island is proved by the requisite number of witnesses, and the court might submit it to the jury whether that assemblage amounted to a levying of war; but the presence of the accused at that assemblage being nowhere alleged except in the indictment, the overt act is not proved by a single witness, and of consequence all other testimony must be irrelevant."

Under the influence of this opinion of the court on the law of the case, the jury brought in a verdict of "not guilty." The prisoner was then arraigned upon an indictment for the misdemeanor; but as the evidence also failed to support that charge, the verdict of the jury was again "not guilty;" whereupon Burr was finally set at liberty, but was required to enter into bail to appear at the ensuing United States court in Ohio to answer to any indictment that might be preferred against him for the offense committed in that State of conspiring to invade the Spanish territory of Mexico. He gave the requisite bail, and was again discharged. This proved, however, to be the end of the prosecution, United States Attorney Hay announcing in open court that he would recommend the executive department to desist from any further pursuit of the merely formal case that now remained.

Thus ended a state trial, the most famous which took place in the United States prior to the impeachment of President Johnson. It could have had no other conclusion in accordance with law. Whether Burr was morally guilty was a question which has been since so much discussed that it cannot be regarded as having been settled by the verdict; but that he was not legally proved to be guilty is certain. The duty of holding the scales of justice even at this trial was the most difficult that Marshall had to encounter during his incumbency on the bench. Jefferson succeeded in importing so much personal feeling and partisanship into the proceedings that the trial wore a very peculiar aspect. There was more in it than party hostility; there was open antagonism between the President of the United States and the Chief Justice; there were also covert and indirect but powerful influences at work in aid of the prosecution. No action of Marshall could have escaped contemporary criticism, and in this case he did not escape it. He was very severely attacked by many persons, who honestly thought that he had done wrong. But the fairer judgment of posterity has given him credit for perfect impartiality, and for sound, even-handed, and courageous administration of the law. The issuing of the subpœna to Jefferson alone remains a controverted point; yet as to this it must be admitted that no authority can be higher or more satisfactory than that of the Chief Justice himself,

CHAPTER XII.

1800–1806.

GENERAL WASHINGTON died on the 14th of December, 1799. By his will, he bequeathed his large collection of valuable papers, private and public, to his nephew, Judge Bushrod Washington. The latter, by much solicitation, induced Judge Marshall to write from these manuscripts the life of Washington. This work, extending, as it did, over more than the previous half century, the most stirring and eventful period of modern history, and filled with events of the most imposing character, necessarily comprised the history of the United States, as well as all the military and civil events leading to the national existence. So much material could not be compressed into moderate limits within a short period. The contract with the publishers to prepare and print the work was dated September 22, 1802, yet four of the five octavo volumes of the work were prepared in manuscript for the press by the

autumn of 1804. The first volume was placed
in the printer's hands in the winter of 1804, and
was actually published in that year. Yet even
this dispatch did not satisfy people at the time.
Indeed, such was the public eagerness for the
book that it was actually looked for before one
page was printed.

Several causes conspired to induce this an-
ticipation. Mr. Jefferson, with characteristic
jealousy, and in his eager anxiety to forestall
any impressions which the publication might
create adverse to his elevation to the presidency
at the next election, — an idea that never entered the mind of Judge Marshall, — sounded
the alarm to his political followers by condemn-
ing the work in advance ; and in his busy correspondence he even covertly imputed these
partisan motives for its early publication.
Among his published letters of that date, two
years before Marshall's first volume appeared,
there is one to his friend Joel Barlow, the author of the " Columbiad," who was then residing at Paris ; to him Jefferson writes : —

" Mr. Madison and myself have cut out a piece of
work for you, which is to write the history of the
United States from the close of the war downwards.
We are rich ourselves in materials, and can open all
the public archives to you ; but your residence here is
essential, because a great deal of the knowledge of

things is not on paper, but only within ourselves for verbal communication. John Marshall is writing the life of General Washington from his papers. It is intended to come out just in time to influence the next presidential election. It is written, therefore, principally with a view to electioneering purposes. It will consequently be out in time to aid you with information, as well as to point out the perversions of truth necessary to be rectified. Think of this and agree to it." [1]

These assertions and these possibly genuine apprehensions of Jefferson were without the least foundation. Judge Washington wrote to Wayne, the publisher, in reference to this suspicion, as follows : —

" The Democrats may say what they please, and I have expected they would say a great deal, but this is, at least, not intended to be a party work, nor will any candid man have cause to make this charge."

The tocsin of alarm, however, thus sounded by Mr. Jefferson, produced an unfavorable influence in the canvass for subscriptions, and combined with the high cost of the volumes to repress the circulation. Judge Washington had anticipated thirty thousand subscribers by the time the first volume went to press. The number actually obtained did not exceed eight thousand.

[1] Jefferson's *Works*, vol. iv. p. 437.

It must be confessed that, whether because he was too much hurried by outside pressure or for some other reason, Marshall did not give himself time to do his work as he might and ought to have done it. The book suffered from haste. The early volumes had an appearance of incompleteness which impaired their value to a degree which, when too late, became mortifying to the author. He, however, frankly acknowledged the justice of this complaint. In the preface to his revised and smaller edition in two volumes, he says: —

"The work was originally composed under circumstances which might afford some apology for its being finished with less care than its importance demanded. The immense mass of papers which it was necessary to read — many of them interesting when written, but no longer so — occupied a great part of that time which the impatience of the public could allow for the appearance of the book itself. It was therefore hurried to the press without that previous careful examination which would have resulted in the correction of some faults that have been since perceived. In the hope of presenting the work to the public in a form more worthy of its acceptance and more satisfactory to himself, the author has given it a careful revision."

Such was the innate modesty of Marshall that he did not intend that his name as author should appear, preferring the mere announcement, " Compiled under the inspection of the Honorable Bushrod Washington from original papers bequeathed to him by his deceased relative." In a letter to Wayne, the publisher, he says : —

" My repugnance to permitting my name to appear in the title still continues, but it shall yield to your right to make the best use you can of the copy. I do not myself imagine that the name of the author being given or withheld can produce any difference in the number of subscribers ; but if you think differently, I should be very unwilling, by a pertinacious adherence to what may be deemed a mere prejudice, to leave you in the opinion that a real injury has been sustained. I have written to Mr. Washington on this subject, and shall submit my scruples to you and him, only requesting my name may not be given. But, on mature consideration and conviction of its propriety, if this shall be ultimately resolved on, I wish not my title in the judiciary of the United States to be annexed to it."

The question thus submitted to Judge Washington was promptly decided. " The Chief Justice," he says, in a letter to Wayne, " with great reluctance consents that his name as author may be inserted in the title-page, provided I insist upon it. It gives me pain to decide against his wishes, but I really think it necessary, for many reasons. It will, I presume, be sufficient to say, ' By John Marshall.' "

The first volume of the work met with the usual varied fortune of commendation and criticism from the public and the press.

In a letter to Wayne, Marshall says : —

" I thank you for the two papers you sent me. The very handsome critique in ' The Political and Commercial Register ' was new to me. I could only regret that there was in it more of panegyric than was merited. The editor of that paper, if the author of the critique, manifests himself to be master of a style of very superior order, and to be, of course, a very correct judge of the compositions of others. . . . I cannot be insensible of the opinions entertained of it, but I am much more solicitous to hear the strictures upon it than to know what parts may be thought exempt from censure. As I am about to give a reading to the first volume, and as not much time can be employed upon it, the strictures of those who were either friendly or hostile to the work may be useful, if communicated to me, because they may direct my attention to defects which might otherwise escape a single reading, however careful that reading may be."

The American press in general spoke favorably of the work as to its accuracy and completeness. Judge Story said: " It could scarcely be doubted that his ' Life of Washington ' would be invaluable for the truth of its facts and the accuracy and completeness of its narrative, and such has been and will continue to be its reputation."[1] Jared Sparks said: "After the able, accurate, and comprehensive work by Chief Justice Marshall it would be presumptuous to attempt a historical biography of Washington."[2] Washington Irving said of it: "Marshall and Sparks are very accurate. Whoever will read the Life by Marshall and the Correspondence by Sparks will have a good idea of Washington."

As to the reception of the work in Great Britain it was hardly to be expected, so soon after the Revolutionary War, that English criticism of such a book should be entirely free from prejudice. The smart of defeat in the successful revolt of the colonies against the mother country was still recent, and rankled in many a British breast. This naturally inspired the harsh spirit in which the book was reviewed in that country. In presenting some extracts from these reviews we forgive, therefore, the bad taste of ungenerous and spiteful criticism, in consideration of the honest admission of the fullness and truth of the biography as a faithful historical narrative.

[1] *National Portrait Gallery*, vol. i.
[2] Allibone's *Dictionary of Authors.*

We quote from the " Edinburgh Review " of October, 1808, as follows : —

" If we are to regard the history of a good man's life as a monument which literature erects to his memory, and consider the magnitude of the intellectual structure as sufficient to insure its celebrity and duration, the Chief Justice of America must certainly be allowed to have graced the fields of literature with one of the most promising trophies ever employed to commemorate the illustrious dead. But mere bulk, we suspect, gives no durable quality to works made of words, and it is not by the space they cover that they are likely to attract the notice of mankind. Mr. Marshall must not, therefore, promise himself a reputation commensurate with the dimensions of his work, for we are greatly afraid that it may come to be superseded, and the name of Washington carried down to posterity by some less ostentatious, but more tasteful and pleasing memorial."

In an article in " Blackwood's Magazine " entitled " American Writers," [1] we read : —

" ' Washington's Life,' " so called, is a great, heavy book that should have been called by some other name. As a lawyer, as a judge, whose decisions, year after year, in the Supreme Court of the United States would have done credit and honor to Westminster Hall in the proud season of English law, we must, we do, revere Chief Justice Marshall. But

---

[1] Nos. 4 and 5, vol. xvii. pp. 57, 187.

we cannot — will not — forgive such a man for hav
ing made such a book about such another man as
George Washington. Full of power, full of truth as
the work undoubtedly is, one gets tired and sick of the
very name of Washington before he gets half through
these four [five] prodigious octavos, which are equal
to about a dozen of our fashionable quartos, — and
all this without finding out by them who Washington
was or what he has done. . . . Insupportably tire-
some, and with all his honesty, care, and sources of
information from the papers of Washington, he is
greatly mistaken several times in matters of importance."

In honesty it must be admitted that the cen-
soriousness of the English critics came nearer
to the truth than the friendly and courteous
compliments of the popular author's countrymen. In the first place, the time had not
come when the life of Washington could be
properly written, so far at least as his administrations as President were concerned. The
questions which had then arisen were too near;
the partisanship was as fresh and as strong as
ever; and even the judicial mind of Marshall
could not escape such powerful present influences. Neither was Marshall altogether fitted
to write a great book; he was not a literary
man nor a scholar; he did not understand the
art of composition, and of making a vivid, con-

densed, attractive narrative. He wrote a useful book, as a man of his ability could not fail
to do when dealing with subjects with which
he was thoroughly familiar, and in which he
was deeply interested; he had further the advantage which arises always from personal
acquaintance with the subject of the memoir
and from entire sympathy with him. For the
student of American history the book must
thus have a value; but general readers have
long since forgotten it, and leave it neglected
on the shelves of the old libraries. It has long
been out of print, and copies of it are not in
demand even by reason of rarity. Jefferson
was so far right in his prognostications concerning it that it is now universally regarded
as a decidedly Federalist biography.

16

THE first Constitution of Virginia was formed in 1776. Though born amid the throes and convulsions of the great Revolutionary strug- gle, it may be doubted whether it has been im- proved upon by any of the several constitutions which have succeeded it. It endured without amendment, in war and in peace, to 1830, a period of more than half a century, and seemed so well adapted to secure the peace and safety of the Commonwealth that many of her wisest citizens greatly lamented when the spirit of in- novation stirred the people to the new fashion of holding a convention and fabricating a suc- cessor to it. John Marshall was one of those who deprecated and opposed the change; but when he found the result inevitable, he wisely resolved to fall in with the popular sentiment, and to aid others of the like faith in an en- deavor to save what was most valuable and dear in the existing order of things.

The Chief Justice, with ex-Presidents Madison and Monroe, and many of the conscript fathers of the republic, became members of the convention. Mr. Monroe was its chosen president, but owing to the increasing feebleness of age was seldom able to preside, and the chair was generally occupied by a skillful parliamentarian in Judge Philip P. Barbour of Orange County, who presided with great acceptance.

A contemporary writer and spectator of the scene has sketched the *personnel* and the leading characters of the convention : —

"Mr. Madison sat on the left of the Speaker; Mr. Monroe, when not in the chair, on the right. Mr. Madison spoke once for half an hour, but although a pin might have been heard to drop, so low was his tone that from the gallery I could distinguish only one word and that was 'constitution.' He stood not more than six feet from the Speaker. When he rose a great part of the members left their seats and clustered round the aged statesman. Mr. Madison was a small man, with an ample forehead and some obliquity of vision (I thought the defect probably of age), his eyes appearing to be slightly introverted. His dress was plain, his overcoat a faded brown surtout. Mr. Monroe was very wrinkled and weatherbeaten, ungraceful in attitude and gesture, and his speeches only commonplace."

Other conspicuous members were, Mr. Giles,

then Governor of the State; Mr. Tazewell, John Randolph of Roanoke, P. P. Barbour, Philip Doddridge of Brooke, Mr. Powell of Frederick, Chapman Johnson of Augusta, and Benjamin Watkins Leigh of Richmond City. The latter made a distinguished figure in the convention, and was armed at all points as the leader of the lowland or eastern party. Judge Marshall is thus described by the writer above quoted: —

"Judge Marshall, whenever he spoke, which was seldom, and for only a short time, attracted great attention. His appearance was Revolutionary and patriarchal. Tall, in a long surtout of blue, with a face of genius and an eye of fire, his mind possessed the rare faculty of condensation; he distilled an argument down to its essence. There were two parties in the house; the western or radical, and the eastern or conservative. Judge Marshall proposed something in the nature of a compromise."[1]

The principal questions which engaged the deliberations of the convention involved the extension of the right of suffrage, the eligibility of government officers by the vote of the people, the readjustment of the basis of representation in the legislature, and the reform of the state judiciary. The particular subject which excited the warmest interest, and which threatened at one time to divide and dismember the

---

[1] Howe's *Virginia Historical Collections*, p. 313.

State, related to the basis of representation in the state legislature. It became at length a sectional and geographical struggle for power; the western part of the State insisting on a purely white basis, and the eastern counties urging a mixed basis founded on a combination of persons and property.

Much irritation prevailed in the debates on these propositions, and serious consequences seemed to threaten the harmony of the Commonwealth. The discussion had lasted through several weeks, with little prospect of agreement. It was in this crisis that the venerable Chief Justice suggested a compromise. He addressed the convention. His voice was somewhat feeble at first, but as he proceeded and grew warm with the patriotic inspiration of his theme, he was distinctly heard throughout the hall; and the manliness, candor, and courtesy of his manner conciliated the confidence of all parties. He said: —

"No person in the house can be more truly gratified than I am at seeing the spirit that has been manifested here to-day; and it is my earnest wish that this spirit of conciliation may be acted upon in a fair, equal, and honest manner, adapted to the situation of the different parts of the Commonwealth which are to be affected. As to the general propositions which have been offered, there is no essential

difference between them. That the Federal numbers and the plan of the white basis shall be blended
together so as to allow each an equal portion of
power seems very generally agreed to. The difference is that one party applies these two principles
separately, the one to the Senate, the other to the
House of Delegates ; while the other party proposes
to unite the two principles, and to carry them in their
blended form through the whole legislature. One
gentleman differs in the whole outline of this plan.
He seems to imagine that we claim nothing of republican principles when we claim a representation
for property. Permit me to set him right. I do
not say that I hope to satisfy him, or others who say
that republican government depends on adopting the
naked principle of numbers, that we are right ; but
I think we can satisfy him that we do entertain a
different opinion. I think the soundest principles of
republicanism do sanction some relation between representation and taxation. Certainly no opinion has
received the sanction of wiser statesmen and patriots.
I think the two ought to be connected. I think this
was the principle of the Revolution, the ground on
which the colonies were torn from the mother country
and made independent states.

"I shall not however go into that discussion now.
The House has already heard much said about it. I
would observe that this basis of representation is a
matter so important to Virginia that the subject was
reviewed by every thinking individual before this
convention assembled. Several different plans were

contemplated. The basis of white population alone; the basis of free population alone; a basis compounded of taxation and white population (or, which is the same thing, a basis of Federal numbers); two other bases were also proposed, one referring to the total population of the State, the other to taxation alone. Now of these various propositions, the basis of white population and the basis of taxation alone are the two extremes. Between the free population and the white population there is almost no difference. Between the basis of total population and the basis of taxation there is but little difference. The people of the east thought that they offered a fair compromise, when they proposed the compound basis of population and taxation, or the basis of the Federal numbers. We thought that we had republican precedent for this — a precedent given us by the wisest and truest patriots that ever were assembled. But that is now past. We are now willing to meet on a new middle ground, beyond what we thought was a middle ground and the extreme on the other side. We considered the Federal numbers as middle ground, and we may, perhaps, now carry that proposition. The gentleman assumed too much when he said that question was decided. It cannot be considered as decided until it has come before the House. The majority is too small to calculate upon it as certain in the final decision. We are all uncertain as to the issue. But all know this, that if either extreme is carried, it must leave a wound in the breast of the opposite party which will fester and rankle and pro-

duce I know not what mischief. The majority also
are now content once more to divide the ground and
to take a new middle ground. The only difficulty is
whether the compromise shall be effected by applying
one principle to the House of Delegates and the
other to the Senate, or by mingling the two principles
and applying them in the same form to both branches
of the legislature. I incline to the latter opinion.
I do not know and have not heard any sufficient
reason assigned for adopting different principles; and
there will be just the same divisions between the two,
as appears in this convention. It can produce no
good, and may, I fear, produce some mischief. It
will be said that one branch is the representation of
one division of the State, and the other branch of another division of it. Ought they not both to represent the whole? Yet I am ready to submit to such
an arrangement, if it shall be the opinion of a majority of this House. If this convention shall think it
best that the House of Delegates shall be organized
in one way and the Senate in another, I shall not
withhold my assent. Give me a constitution that
shall be received by the people; a constitution in
which I can consider their different interests to be
duly represented, and I will take it, though it may
not be that I most approve.

" The principle, then, which I propose as a compromise is, that the apportionment of representation
shall be made according to an exact compound of
the two principles of the white basis and of the
Federal numbers according to the census of 1820."

· There was a considerable discussion, following Judge Marshall's speech. The "exact compound" would have given, as was said, the whole white population and three tenths of the colored, whether bond or free. When Judge Marshall again addressed the convention, his speech, though brief, " was at the time regarded as an unrivaled specimen of lucid and conclusive reasoning." [1]

" Two propositions," he said, " respecting the basis of representation have divided this convention almost equally. One party has supported the basis of white population alone, the other has supported a basis compounded of white population and taxation, — or, which is the same thing in its results, the basis of Federal numbers. The question has been discussed until discussion has become useless. It has been argued until argument is exhausted. We have now met on the ground of compromise. . . . One party proposes that the House of Delegates shall be formed on the basis of white population exclusively, and the Senate on the mixed basis of white population and taxation, or on the Federal numbers. The other party proposes that the white population shall be combined with Federal numbers, and shall, mixed in equal proportions, form the basis of representation in both Houses. This last proposition must be equal. All feel it to be equal. If the two principles are combined exactly, and, thus combined, form the basis

[1] *Southern Literary Messenger*, vol. ii. p. 188.

of both Houses, the compromise must be perfectly
equal. . . .

"After the warm language (to use the mildest
phrase) which has been mingled with argument on
both sides, I heard with inexpressible satisfaction
propositions for compromise proposed by both parties
in the language of conciliation. I hail these auspi-
cious appearances with as much joy as the inhabitant
of the polar regions hails the reappearance of the
sun after his long absence of six tedious months.
Can these appearances prove fallacious? Is it a
meteor we have seen and mistaken for that splendid
luminary which dispenses light and gladness throughout creation? It must be so, if we cannot meet on
equal ground. If we cannot meet on the line that
divides us equally, then take the hand of friendship
and make an *equal* compromise, it is vain to hope
that *any* compromise can be made."

The wise and conciliatory terms for com-
promising the formidable disputes which had
grown out of the discussion of the basis question, especially the candid spirit in which Marshall presented those terms, led to a better
temper in the convention, and powerfully con-
duced to the acceptance of the form of settle-
ment which was finally adopted and incorporated into the new constitution. It was upon
the grand principle of mutual concession that
the Chief Justice yielded at length his cordial
assent to that instrument, though many of its

provisions were in opposition to his settled convictions.

The question of changing the manner of appointing the judges and magistrates of the
Commonwealth, and their tenure of office, naturally awakened earnest solicitude in the mind
of the Chief Justice. On this subject he spoke
with unwonted earnestness and power. He
was especially desirous to preserve the county
court system of Virginia, — a system, by the
way, which was regarded by Mr. Jefferson
with great aversion : —

" The justices of these courts," said the latter,
" are self-chosen, are for life, and perpetuate their
own body in succession forever, so that a faction
once possessing themselves of the bench of a county
can never be broken up, but hold their county in
chains forever indissoluble. Yet these justices are
the real executive, as well as judiciary, in all our
minór and most ordinary concerns. They tax us at
will, and fill the office of sheriff. . . . The juries —
our judges of all fact, and of the law when they choose
it — are not selected by the people nor amenable to
them. They are chosen by an officer named by the
court and executive." [1]

Judge Marshall, on the contrary, well versed
in the practical operation and the wholesome
conservative influence exerted by these tribu-

[1] Jefferson's *Works:* Letter to Samuel Kerchival, July, 1816.

nals, earnestly advocated their preservation and a continuance in the present mode of appointing the justices. He said : —

" I am not in the habit of bestowing extravagant eulogies upon my countrymen ; I would rather hear them pronounced by others ; but it is a truth that no State in the Union has hitherto enjoyed more complete internal quiet than Virginia. There is no part of America where less disquiet and less ill-feeling between man and man is to be found, than in this Commonwealth ; and I believe most firmly that this state of things is mainly to be ascribed to the practical operation of our county courts. The magistrates who compose those courts consist in general of the best men in their respective counties. They act in the spirit of peacemakers, and allay rather than excite the small disputes and differences which will sometimes arise among neighbors. It is certainly much owing to this that so much harmony prevails amongst us. These courts must be preserved ; if we part with them, can we be sure that we shall retain among our justices of the peace the same respectability and weight of character as are now to be found ? I think not. . . .

" I have grown old in the opinion that there is nothing more dear to Virginia, or that ought to be dearer to her statesmen, and that the best interests of our country are secured by it. Advert, sir, to the duties of a judge. He has to pass between the government and the man whom that government is pros·

ecuting; between the most powerful individual in
the community and the poorest and most unpopular.
It is of the last importance that, in the exercise of
these duties, he should observe the utmost fairness.
Need I press the necessity of this ? Does not every
man feel that his own personal security and the security of his property depend on that fairness? The
judicial department comes home, in its effects, to
every man's fireside; it passes on his property, his
reputation, his life, his all. Is it not to the last degree important that he should be rendered perfectly
and completely independent, with nothing to influence
or control him but God and his conscience? . . .
We have heard about sinecures and judicial pen-
sioners. Sir, the weight of such terms is well known
here. To avoid creating a sinecure you take away
a man's duties when he wishes them to remain; you
take away the duty of one man and give it to another; and this is a sinecure. What is this in substance but saying that there is and can be and ought
to be no such thing as judicial independence. . . .
I have always thought, from my earliest youth until
now, that the greatest scourge an angry Heaven
ever inflicted upon an ungrateful and sinning people
was an ignorant, a corrupt, or a dependent judiciary.
Our ancestors thought so; we thought so till very
lately; and I trust the vote of this day will show
that we think so still. Will you draw down this
curse on Virginia ? "

The Chief Justice was now seventy-five years
of age, and this service in the Virginia Conven-

tion closed his political life. But, though somewhat enfeebled physically by age and infirmity, he retained and actively discharged the duties of his judicial office until his death, like Moses, with " his eye not dimmed nor his natural force abated."

CHAPTER XIV.

OPINIONS: PERSONAL TRAITS.

1832–1835.

JUDGE MARSHALL'S opinions on the question of slavery were formed with deliberation and were well known. Though a slave-holder himself by inheritance, he felt the institution to be a plague-spot on the body politic, which he earnestly desired to see eradicated. He understood, however, the bearings of the subject too well to entertain any sympathy with the schemes of instantaneous abolition, which fanatical intermeddlers urged so persistently, without pausing to reflect on the dreadful consequences which would ensue from the two races occupying the same territory in natural and inevitable antagonism, under that plan of emancipation. He believed that, as a peaceful remedy, it would in the condition of the country at that time have proved a failure, and have issued in the bitter hostility of the races, and the almost certain destruction, ultimately, of the colored population. The experience of

Great Britain in such a scheme of emancipation in her West India colonies, with the example of the San Domingo massacres as a warning, held out no hope of good results in our slave States. This strengthened his conviction that unless a scheme of voluntary deportation, as proposed by the Colonization Society, should prove successful, the evil was incurable except by some such destructive convulsion as civil war. He was therefore the strong and ardent advocate of the objects of that society, and favored the plan of state aid and coöperation, and of dedicating the entire proceeds of the sale of the public lands of the United States to the purchase and transportation of the slave population to Africa. On this subject he urged his views with great force.

" It is undoubtedly of great importance," he said, " to retain the countenance and protection of the general government. Some of our cruisers stationed on the coast of Africa would at the same time interrupt the slave-trade, a horrid traffic detested by all good men, and would protect the vessels and commerce of the colony from pirates who infest those seas. The power of the government to afford this aid is not, I believe, contested. I regret that its power to grant pecuniary aid is not equally free from question. On this subject I have always thought and still think that the proposition made by Mr. King in the Senate is the most unexceptionable and the most effective that can be devised. . . . The lands are the property of the United States, and have hitherto been disposed of by the government under the idea of absolute ownership."[1]

Judge Marshall took no active part in the political controversies of the day, nor of course could he properly do so, though he was not without a warm interest respecting them. He lamented, even with gloom and despondency, the ascendency of principles in Virginia which he believed, if carried into practice, would lead to civil war and too probably involve the overthrow of the government. In a letter to Judge Story, written two years before his death, in which he acknowledged the receipt of Story's "Commentaries on the Constitution," which had been dedicated to him, he says: —

"I have just finished reading your great work, and wish it could be read by every statesman and every would-be statesman in the United States. It is a comprehensive and an accurate commentary on our Constitution, formed in the spirit of the original text. In the South we are so far gone in political meta-physics that I fear no demonstration can restore us to common sense. The words ' State Rights,' as expounded by the Resolutions of 1798, and the Report

---

[1] *Fifteenth Annual Report of the Colonization Society,* p. 32 Letter from Marshall, Dec. 14, 1831.

of 1799, construed by our legislature, have a charm
against which all reasouing is vain. Those resolutions and that report constitute the creed of every
politician who hopes to rise in Virginia ; and to question them, or even to adopt the construction given by
their author,[1] is deemed political sacrilege. The solemn and interesting admonitions of your concluding
remarks will not, I fear, avail as they ought to avail
against this popular frenzy.

I am grateful for the very flattering terms in which
you speak of your friend in many parts of this valuable work as well as in the dedication. In despite
of my vanity I cannot suppress the fear that you will
be supposed by others, as well as myself, to have consulted a partial friendship farther than your deliberate judgment will approve. Others may not contemplate this partiality with as much gratification as its
object." [2]

While the Chief Justice was opposed to the
general principles of President Jackson's administration in 1832–33, he most heartily approved the President's bold and vigorous treatment of the nullification heresy, which threatened civil war and imperiled the safety of the
Union. He cordially approved the proclamation of the President and the Force Bill enacted by Congress, both leveled at the dangerous dogma which was enacted into law by

[1] Mr. Madison.
[2] Story's *Life and Letters,* vii. p. 135 ; July 31, 1833.

the State of South Carolina. With Judge Marshall, both nullification and secession were utterly subversive of all stable government, and at open war with its organic principles and objects. Judge Story, speaking of a dinner at the President's at the time of the debate on the Force Bill, says : —

" I forgot to say that, notwithstanding 'I am the most dangerous man in America,'[1] the President specially invited me to drink a glass of wine with him. But what is more remarkable, since his last proclamation and message the Chief Justice and myself have become his warmest supporters, and shall continue so just as long as he maintains the principles contained in them. Who would have dreamed of such an occurrence? "[2]

Marshall's health was naturally good, and being of simple, regular, and temperate habits, he suffered little from sickness of any kind. We are indebted to his grandson, John Marshall, Esq., of Markham, for the following interesting letter from the Chief Justice, found among the letters of his son, the late Edward C. Marshall, hitherto unpublished : —

" WASHINGTON, *Feb.* 15, 1832.

"MY DEAR SON, — Your letter of the 10th gave me great pleasure, because it assured me of the health

---

[1] So called by General Jackson.
[2] Story's *Life and Letters*, vol. ii. p. 117.

of your family and the health of the other families in which I take so deep an interest. My own has improved. I strengthen considerably, and am able, without fatigue, to walk to court, a distance of two miles, and return to dinner. At first this exercise was attended with some difficulty, but I feel no inconvenience from it now. The sympathetic feeling to which you allude has sustained no diminution; I fear it never will. I perceive no symptoms, and I trust I never shall, of returning disease.

"The question on Mr. Van Buren's nomination [1] was not exempt from difficulty. Those who opposed him, I believe, thought conscientiously that his appointment ought not to be confirmed. They feel a great hostility to that gentleman from other causes than his letter to Mr. McLane. They believe him to have been at the bottom of a system which they condemn. Whether this conviction be well or ill founded, it is their conviction, — at least I believe it is. In such a case it is extremely difficult, almost impossible, for any man to separate himself from his party.

"This session of Congress is indeed peculiarly interesting. The discussions on the tariff and on the Bank, especially, will, I believe, call forth an unusual display of talents. I have no hope that any accommodation can take place on the first question. The bitterness of party spirit on that subject threatens to continue unabated. There seems to be no prospect of allaying it.

[1] As minister to England.

" The two great objects in Virginia are internal improvement and our colored population. On the first, I despair. On the second, we might do much if our unfortunate political prejudices did not restrain us from asking the aid of the Federal Government. As far as I can judge, that aid, if asked, would be freely and liberally given.

" The association you speak of, if it could be made extensive, might be of great utility. I would suggest the addition of a resolution not to bring any slave within the country. My love to ——.

" I am, my dear son,

" Your affectionate father,

" J. MARSHALL."

" To Mr. E. C. MARSHALL."

It was only in the year 1831, when he was seventy-six years of age, that Judge Marshall was attacked with any serious disease. Then he became the victim of that cruel malady, the stone. His recovery from a severe surgical operation was attributed by one of his physicians " to his extraordinary self-possession, and to the calm and philosophical views which he took of his case."

Although he was restored to health and shared the great joy of his friends and family on that account, the unseen shadow of a great calamity was impending over him, which too soon caused him to realize in sadness the impressive words of the poet : —

"The spider's most attenuated thread
Is cord, is cable, to man's tender tie
On earthly bliss; it breaks at every breeze."

This heavy misfortune was the death of his wife, to whom he was so ardently attached, and which followed closely upon his own restoration to health, taking place December 25, 1831. He was devoted to her, and felt her loss with the keenest anguish. She had suffered much and long from continued ill - health, and, as Bishop Meade remarks, the tender and assiduous attention he paid to her was the most interesting and striking feature in his domestic character. "She was nervous in the extreme. The least noise was sometimes agony to her whole frame, and his perpetual endeavor was to keep the house and yard and out-houses from the slightest cause of distressing her; walking, himself, at times, about the house and yard without shoes. On one occasion, when she was in her most distressing state, the town authorities of Richmond manifested their great respect for him and sympathy for her by having either the town clock or town bell muffled." [1]

Judge Story, who saw much of him at this time, afterward said: "She must have been a very extraordinary woman, so to have attached him; and I think he is the most extraordinary

[1] *Old Churches and Families of Virginia,* vol. ii. p. 222.

man I ever saw, for the depth and tenderness of his feelings." [1]

At the beginning of the next term of the Supreme Court, January, 1833, the Chief Justice was present, and although now in his seventy-eighth year his health seemed excellent. "The court opened on Monday last," says Judge Story, "and all the judges were present, except Judge Baldwin. All were in good health, and the Chief Justice seemed to revive and enjoy anew his green old age. He brought with him and presented to each of us a copy of the new edition of the Life of Washington, inscribing on the fly page of mine a very kind remark. . . . Having some leisure on our hands, the Chief Justice and myself have devoted some of it to attendance upon the theatre to hear Miss Fanny Kemble, who has been in the city the past week. We attended on Monday night, and on the Chief Justice's entrance into the box he was cheered in a marked manner. He behaved as he always does, with extreme modesty, and seemed not to know that the compliment was designed for him. We have seen Miss Kemble as Julia in ' The Hunchback,' and as Mrs. Haller in ' The Stranger.' . . . I have never seen any female acting at all comparable to hers. She is so graceful that you forget that

[1] Story's *Life and Letters:* Letter to Mrs. Story, vol. ii. p. 86.

she is not very handsome. In Mrs. Haller she threw the whole audience into tears. The Chief Justice shed them in common with younger eyes." [1]

As to Judge Marshall's religious opinions and character, no man can speak with more accuracy and authority than the venerable Bishop Meade, who, as an Episcopal clergyman first, and afterward Bishop of the Episcopal Church of Virginia, knew him more intimately in these ecclesiastical relations than any of his contemporaries. It is sufficiently obvious, from what has already been told of the simplicity of Marshall's character and the benevolence of his life, that there were no materials in his mind or character out of which an atheist or an infidel could have been made. The Bishop writes: "I can never forget how he would prostrate his tall form before the rude low benches without backs at Cool Spring meeting-house, in the midst of his children and grandchildren and his neighbors. In Richmond he always set an example to the gentlemen of the same conformity, though many of them did not follow it. He not only conformed to the ceremonies of religion, but his whole life evinced virtuous principles and affections. He was a sincere friend to religion, and a constant attendant

---

[1] Story's *Life and Letters,* vol. vii. p. 116.

upon its ministrations. Brought up in the Episcopal Church, he adhered to it through life; though not until a short time before his death a believer in its fundamental doctrines."

His daughter, during her last illness, said: —

" The reason why he never communed was, that he was a Unitarian in opinion, though he never joined their society. He told her he believed in the truth of the Christian Revelation, but not in the divinity of Christ; therefore he could not commune in the Episcopal Church. But during the last months of his life he read ' Keith on Prophecy,' where our Saviour's divinity is incidentally treated, and was convinced by this work, and the fuller investigation to which it led, of the supreme divinity of the Saviour. He determined to apply for admission to the communion of our Church, objected to communion in private, because he thought it his duty to make a public confession of the Saviour; and while waiting for improved health to enable him to go to the church for that purpose, he grew worse and died, without ever communing."

In this connection, and in illustration of the depth and fervor of his religious convictions, the following authentic anecdote is of interest. He was once traveling in the northern part of Virginia, and about nightfall arrived at the village of Winchester in Frederick County. He drove to what was then known as Mc-

Guire's Hotel. What occurred there has been thus related : —

" A gentleman was traveling in one of the counties in Virginia, and about the close of the day stopped at a public house to obtain refreshment and spend the night. He had been there but a short time before an old man alighted from his gig, with the apparent intention of becoming his fellow-guest at the same house. As the old man drove up, the traveler observed that both the shafts of his gig were broken, and that they were held together by withes formed from the bark of a hickory sapling. He observed also that he was plainly clad, that his knee-buckles were loosened, and that something like negligence pervaded his dress. Conceiving him to be one of the honest yeomanry of our land, the courtesies of strangers passed between them, and they entered the tavern. About the same time an addition of three or four young gentlemen was made to their number, — most, if not all of them, of the legal profession. As soon as they became conveniently accommodated, the conversation was turned by one of the latter upon an eloquent harangue which had that day been displayed at the bar. It was replied by another that he had witnessed on the same day a degree of eloquence no doubt equal, but it was from the pulpit ; and a warm and able altercation ensued, in which the merits of the Christian religion became the subject of discussion. From six o'clock until eleven the young champions wielded the sword of argument, adducing with ingenuity and

ability everything that could be said *pro* and *con.*
During this protracted period the old gentleman list-
ened with all the meekness and modesty of a child,
as if he was adding new information to the stores
of his own mind. . . .

" At last one of the young men, remarking that it
was impossible to combat with long established prejudices, wheeled about, and, with some familiarity, ex-
claimed: 'Well, my old gentleman, what think you of
these things?' 'If,' said the traveler, 'a streak of
vivid lightning had at that moment crossed the room,
their amazement could not have been greater than
it was with what followed.' The most eloquent and
unanswerable appeal was made for nearly an hour
by the old gentleman, that he ever heard or read.
So perfect was his recollection, that every argument
urged against the Christian religion was met in the
order in which it was advanced. Hume's sophistry
on the subject of miracles was, if possible, more perfectly answered than it had already been by Campbell. And in the whole lecture there was so much
simplicity and energy, pathos and sublimity, that not
another word was uttered. ' An attempt to describe
it,' said the traveler, ' would be an attempt to paint
the sunbeams.' It was now a matter of curiosity and
inquiry who the old gentleman was. The traveler
concluded it was the preacher from whom the pulpit
eloquence was heard; but no, it was the *Chief Justice of the United States.*" [1]

[1] This account was originally published in the Winchester
Republican, but is preserved in durable form in Howe's *Virginia Historical Collections*, p. 275.

The residence of the Chief Justice in Richmond, built by himself, and situated on Shockhoe Hill, yet stands between Marshall and Clay
streets, the former street being named after
him, and is owned and occupied by his descendants.   Without any architectural pretensions, it is a large and commodious brick man-
sion, originally situated upon an ample lot of
about two acres.   His judicial labors were so
arranged that he spent much of the year at
home.   The session of the Supreme Court at
Washington and of the circuit courts of Virginia and North Carolina comprised the annual
round of his official duties.

" Having thus some leisure, and being fond of agriculture, he purchased a farm three or four miles
from Richmond, in Henrico County, which he visited
frequently, often on foot.   He retained also the Oak
Hill estate in Fauquier County, to which he made an
annual visit.   His family and social attachments were
warm and constant, and these visits to Fauquier were
always highly enjoyed both by himself and his numerous relatives and friends."

He was so full of genuine benevolence and
good-will that his hand, heart, and purse were
ever ready for a kindness, and he was an active
member of numerous societies whose mission it
was to do good.   He belonged for nearly half a
tentury to the *Amicable Society* at Richmond,

which was formed to relieve strangers and way-farers in distress, for whom the law made no provision. He was a member of the *Masonic Order.* He belonged to the *Colonization Society*, and took an active interest in its objects. He was a prominent officer of the *Virginia Bible Society*, and was a friend to the Sunday-schools. Once he walked at the head of the procession of these schools through the streets of Richmond, in token of his earnest sympathy in their cause. He was a pew-owner in the Monumental Episcopal Church, and a regular attendant on its services.

The Chief Justice was a great admirer of the ladies, whose society he greatly enjoyed. He always warmly defended their equality in native intellect with the sterner sex. He was remarkable also for his fondness for children and young men. He took an active interest in their sports and exercises, and was always a favorite with them.

" He was a most conscientious man," says Bishop Meade, " in regard to some things which others might regard as too trivial to be observed. It was my privilege more than once to travel with him between Fauquier and Fredericksburg, when we were both going to the lower country. On one occasion, the roads being in their worst condition, when we came to that most miry part called the ' Black Jack,' he found that the travelers through it had taken a nearer and better road through a plantation, the fence being down or very low. I was proceeding to pass over; but he said we had better go round, although each step was a plunge; adding that it was his duty, as one in office, to be very particular in regard to such things. As to some other matters, however, he was not so particular. Although myself never much given to dress or equipage, I was not at all ashamed to compare with him during these travels, whether as to clothing, horse, saddle, or bridle. Servant he had none. Federalist as he was in politics, in his manners and habits he was truly Republican. Would that all republicans were like him in this respect. . . . On one of my visits to Richmond, being in a street near his house, between daybreak and sunrise, I met him on horseback, with a bag of clover seed lying before him, which he was carrying to his farm, it being the time of sowing such seed." [1]

Although his great modesty and the natural reserve of his manners in society might be supposed to render him somewhat morose, Judge Marshall was of an extremely cheerful, even hilarious, disposition, and greatly enjoyed the society of persons congenial to him. He was a member of the Barbecue or Quoit Club at Richmond for more than forty years, and always participated in the exercise and recreation that took place at their meetings with the zest

[1] *Old Churches and Families of Virginia*, vol. ii. p. 222.

of true enjoyment. This famous club was formed in 1788, and consisted of thirty members. They met once a fortnight from May until October, near Buchanan's Spring, about a mile from the city. A visitor, who was present at a meeting of the club in the lifetime of the Chief Justice, has given the following account of it: —

" The club consists of judges, lawyers, doctors, and merchants, — and the Governor of the Commonwealth has a general invitation, when he enters into office.

" On the day I was present, dinner was ready at half-past three o'clock, and consisted of excellent meats and fish, well prepared and well served, with the vegetables of the season. Your veritable *gourmand* never fails to regale himself on his favorite *barbecue*, which is a fine fat pig called a *shoat*, cooked on or over the coals and highly seasoned with cayenne. A dessert of melons and fruits follows, and punch, porter, and toddy are the table liquors ; but with the fruits comes on the favorite beverage of the Virginians, — mint-julep, in place of wine. I never witnessed more festivity and good humor than prevailed at this club. By the constitution, the subject of politics is forbidden. . . . It was refreshing to see such a man as Chief Justice Marshall laying aside the reserve of his dignified stations and contending with the young men at a game of quoits, with all the emulation of youth.

" Many anecdotes are told of occurrences at these meetings. Such is the partiality for the Chief Justice, that it is said the greatest anxiety is felt for his success in the game by by-standers; and on one occasion an old Scotch gentleman was called on to decide between his quoit and that of another member, who, after seemingly careful measurement, announced ' *Mister Mareshall has it a leattle*,' when it was visible to all that the contrary was the case. A French gentleman (Baron Quenet) was at one time a guest when the Governor, the Chief Justice, and several of the judges of the High Court of Appeals were engaged with others, *with coats off*, in a well-contested game. He asked if it was possible that the dignitaries of the land could thus intermix with private citizens ; and when assured of the fact he observed, with true Gallican enthusiasm, that ' he had never before seen the real beauty of republicanism.' . . .

" Judge Marshall was very punctual in his attendance at the club, and no one contributed more to the pleasantness of their meetings. Even as years advanced he was among the most skillful in throwing the *discus*, as he was in discussion ; . . . and it delighted his competitors as much as himself to see him *ring the meg*. He would hurl his iron ring of two pounds' weight with rarely erring aim fifty-five or sixty feet ; — and at some *chef d'œuvre* of skill, in himself or his partner, would spring up and clap his hands with all the light-hearted enthusiasm of boyhood. In his yearly visits to Fauquier, where the proper implements of his sport were not to be had, he still practiced it among his rustic friends with flat stones for quoits.

"A casual guest at a *barbecue* — one of those rural entertainments so frequent among the people of Virginia — saw, soon after his arrival at the spot, an old man emerge from a thicket which bordered the neighboring brook, carrying as large a pile of these flat stones as he could hold between his right arm and his chin. He stepped briskly up to the company and threw down his load among them, saying, ' There! here are quoits enough for us all.' The stranger's surprise may be imagined when he found that this plain and cheerful old man was the Chief Justice of the United States."

Judge Marshall was an early riser, and was often seen returning from market at sunrise with poultry in one hand and a basket of vegetables in the other. It is related that while in the market, on one occasion, a young man, who had recently removed to Richmond, was fretting and swearing violently because he could find no one to take home his turkey. Marshall stepped up and offered to take the turkey home for him. Arriving at the house, the young man inquired "What shall I pay you?" "Oh, nothing," was the reply; "it was on my way, and no trouble." As Marshall walked away, the other inquired of a by-stander, — "Who is that polite old man that brought home my turkey for me?" "That," was the reply, " is Judge Marshall, Chief Justice of the United States."

No man was more just or more generous. Of this we cite a single example. In passing through Culpeper, on his way to Fauquier, he fell in company, at a tavern on the roadside, with Mr. S., an old brother officer of the army of the Revolution. In the course of conversation, Marshall learned that there was a mortgage on the estate of his friend to the amount of $3,000, which was about to fall due. The old gentleman was unable to raise the sum, and was greatly distressed at the prospect of impending ruin. Before parting from him, Marshall privately left a check for the amount with the landlord, which was presented to Mr. S. after Marshall's departure. Impelled by a chivalrous feeling of independence, Mr. S. mounted and spurred his horse until he overtook the judge, and then, with thanks, sought to decline the generosity. But Marshall strenuously persisted ; and finally there was a compromise, by which Marshall took security on the loan ; but he was never known to call for the money. [1]

The fame and popularity of the Chief Justice naturally attracted to him the attention of

[1] Howe's *Virginia Historical Collections,* p. 266.

foreign visitors to this country. Among others, Miss Martineau met him at Washington in the winter preceding his death. She said of him : —

" With Judge Story sometimes came the man to whom he looked up with feelings little short of adoration, — the aged Chief Justice Marshall. There was almost too much mutual respect in our first meeting; we knew something of his individual merits and services, and he maintained through life and carried to his grave a reverence for woman, as rare in its kind as in its degree. It had all the theoretical fervor and magnificence of Uncle Toby's, with the advantage of being grounded upon an extensive knowledge of the sex. He was the father and grandfather of woman ; and out of this experience he brought, not only the love and pity which their offices and position command, and the awe and purity which they excite in the minds of the pure, but a steady conviction of their intellectual equality with men, and with this a deep sense of their social injuries. Throughout life he so invariably sustained their cause that no indulgent libertine dared to flatter and humor, no skeptic, secure in the possession of power, dared to scoff at the claims of woman in the presence of Marshall, who, made clear-sighted by his purity, knew the sex far better than either.

" How delighted we were to see Judge Story bring in the tall, majestic, bright-eyed old man, — old by chronology, by the lines on his composed face, and by his services to the republic; but so dignified, so fresh, so present to the time, that no feeling of compassionate consideration for age dared to mix with the contemplation of him.

" The first evening he asked me much about English politics, and especially whether the people were not fast ripening for the abolition of our religious establishment, — an institution which, after a long study of it, he considered so monstrous 'n principle, and so injurious to true religion in practice, that he could not imagine that it could be upheld for anything but political purposes. There was no prejudice here on account of American modes being different; for he observed that the clergy were, there as elsewhere, far from being in the van of society, and lamented the existence of much fanaticism in the United States; but he saw the evils of an establishment, the more clearly, not the less, from being aware of the faults in the administration of religion at home. The most animated moment of our conversation was when I told him I was going to visit Mr. Madison on leaving Washington. IIe instantly sat upright in his chair, and with beaming eyes began to praise Mr. Madison. Madison received the mention of Marshall's name in just the same manner; yet these men were strongly opposed in politics, and their magnanimous appreciation of each other underwent no slight or brief trial." [1]

From another English traveler, who met the

---

[1] Martineau's *Western Travel*, English ed., vol. i. p. 247.

Chief Justice in Richmond, we have the following sketch :—

"The judge is a tall, venerable man, about eighty
years of age, his hair tied in a queue, and with a countenance indicating that simplicity of mind and benig-
nity which so eminently distinguish his character.
As a judge he has no rival, — his knowledge being
profound, his judgment clear and just, and his quick-
ness in apprehending either the fallacy or truth of
an argument surprising. I had the pleasure of several long conversations with him, and was struck with
admiration at the extraordinary union of modesty
and power, gentleness and force, which his mind displays. What he knows he communicates without
reserve; he speaks with clearness of expression and
in a tone of simple truth which compels conviction;
and on all subjects on which his knowledge is not
certain, or which admit of doubt or argument, he
delivers his opinion with candid diffidence, and with
a deference to that of others amounting almost to
timidity; still, it is a timidity that would disarm the
most violent opponent, and win respect and credence
from any auditor. I remember having often observed a similar characteristic attributed to the im-
mortal Newton. The simplicity of his character is
not more singular than that of his life: pride, os-
tentation, and hyprocrisy are *Greek* to him; and he
really lives up to the letter and spirit of republicanism,
while he maintains all the dignity due to his age and
office. . . . I verily believe there is not a particle of

vanity in his composition, unless it be of that venial and hospitable nature which induces him to pride himself on giving to his friends the best glass of Madeira in Virginia. In short, blending as he does the simplicity of a child and the plainness of a republican with the learning and ability of a lawyer, the venerable dignity of his appearance would not suffer in comparison with that of the most respected and distinguished looking peer in the British House of Lords." [1]

[1] *Travels in North America*, by the Hon. Charles Augustus Murray, vol. i. p. 158.

CHAPTER XV.

THE death of Chief Justice Marshall, which occurred in Philadelphia on the 6th day of July, 1835, in the eightieth year of his age, created a profound impression throughout the country. His long career of public service, his extensive learning, his clear and massive intellect, his incorruptible integrity, and his profound wisdom, united to the simplicity of his character and the genial kindness of his disposition and manners, had made his name a synonym of true greatness and himself a favorite with all classes of men. Thus his death, though not unexpected, was everywhere deplored as a public calamity, and every possible form of respect and sympathy was everywhere displayed.

At the session of the Supreme Court in the winter of 1835 it was manifest that his health was declining. He suffered much pain through the spring, and, at the earnest solicitation of his family and friends, he revisited Philadelphia to seek the relief which had formerly been afforded him by the medical skill of that city. He was accompanied by three of his sons; and during his illness he received every consolation from filial attention, and from the kindness of his numerous friends in Philadelphia, who showed the deepest interest in his situation, and did all in their power for his relief. The famous Dr. Physic stated that —

"The cause of his death was a very diseased condition of the liver, which was enormously enlarged, and contained several tuberculous abscesses of great size. Its pressure upon the stomach had the effect of dislodging this organ from its natural situation, and compressing it in such a manner that for some time previous to his death it would not retain the smallest quantity of nutriment." [1]

He was fully conscious of his approaching end, which he met with perfect composure. His intellect was unclouded to the last moment. A few days before his death, and in full view of it, he wrote with characteristic modesty the following inscription for his tomb: —

"John Marshall, son of Thomas and Mary Marshall, was born on the 24th of September, 1755; intermarried with Mary Willis Ambler the 3d of January, 1783; departed this life — day of —— 18 —."

On Monday, the 6th of July, 1835, about

[1] Randolph's *Memoir of Dr. Physic*, p. 101.

six o'clock in the evening, he died without a struggle.

The event elicited everywhere manifestations of deep sorrow. The citizens of Philadelphia assembled in public meeting to express their sentiments on the occasion. The venerable Bishop White, then in the eighty-eighth year of his age, presided, and appropriate resolutions were adopted. A committee of the Philadelphia bar accompanied his remains to Richmond, where they were met by an immense procession formed of the military, the judges and officers of the courts, the members of the bar, the Masonic fraternity, the civil authorities, and the citizens *en masse.* Thus the funeral *cortège* was escorted to his residence, where the last services were performed by the aged and venerated Bishop Moore, of the Episcopal Church, in a fervent and feeling manner. He was buried by the side of his wife in what was then called the New Burying-Ground, now Shockhoe Hill Cemetery. As the sad news of his decease spread through the country, meetings were held and resolutions of sympathy and sorrow were adopted, not only in the large cities and towns, but at the court-houses and villages throughout the land. In Richmond especially, where he was best known and most loved, the sorrow of the citizens was unbounded.

As his death occurred during the summer vacation of the courts, no opportunity occurred to offer in an official form a memorial tribute of respect, until the 23d of November, 1835. On that day a meeting of the judges, members of the bar, and officers of the Circuit Court of the United States for the Eastern District of Virginia was held in the court-room in the city of Richmond. The Hon. Philip Pendleton Barbour presided, and a preamble and resolutions were proposed by Benjamin Watkins Leigh, Esq., and unanimously adopted.

The Supreme Court of the United States, at its session of January 12, 1836, observed the like customary and sad formalities. At the meeting Edmund I. Lee, Esq., was chairman, General Walter Jones was secretary, Henry Clay offered the resolutions, and Judge Story spoke concerning his associate, for whom he had felt an exceptional affection and admiration.

At a meeting of the social club at Buchanan's Spring, when there was a motion to supply the vacancy occasioned by the death of Judge Marshall, Mr. B. Watkins Leigh proposed as appropriate that "there should be no attempt to fill it ever; but that the number of the club should remain one less than it was before his death."

The death of the Chief Justice was also appropriately memorialized by numerous addresses and discourses before learned societies and public institutions. Among these, and possessing peculiar merit from their elegance and beauty, were Judge Story's discourse on his life, character, and services, delivered at the request of the Suffolk bar in Massachusetts; Mr. Horace Binney's eulogy, delivered at the request of the councils of Philadelphia; and the memoir by Mr. Joseph Hopkinson, pronounced before the " American Philosophical Society," at Philadelphia.

Half a century has elapsed since the death of Chief Justice Marshall, but there is no token of any waning of the respect and affection entertained for his memory by the American people. Almost as we write these lines, the most recent manifestation of the grateful remembrance of his countrymen is shown in the unveiling, at the national capital, of Story's statue of the great Chief Justice, amid the sincere display of popular enthusiasm.

The Commonwealth of Virginia, desirous of perpetuating in some enduring form the memory of her sons, who, under the providence of God, were instrumental with their compatriots in achieving and consolidating the liberties of our country in the great Revolutionary struggle of 1776, took steps some years ago to erect on her Capitol Square in Richmond a colossal group of statuary in bronze, surmounted by an equestrian statue of Washington, exhibiting separately, on a circle of pedestals, the statues of Jefferson, Henry, Marshall, Nelson, Lewis, and Mason. This design was happily executed in part by Thomas Crawford, the American sculptor, and completed by Randolph Rogers of New York.

INDEX.